OPERATOR 5:
INVASION FROM THE SKY

SECRET SERVICE OPERATOR #5™
AMERICA'S UNDERCOVER ACE

INVASION
FROM THE SKY

By Curtis Steele

POPULAR PUBLICATIONS • 2025

CHAPTER 1
FLAMING NIGHT

JIMMY CHRISTOPHER'S keen blue eyes flickered to the clock-face on the dashboard of his speeding coupé, and the frown of annoyance deepened between his slightly puckered brows. Almost eight o'clock, and he was still a good half-hour from his destination. The thought of that destination made his expression grim with concern.

Everything had seemed to happen to him that afternoon; everything had conspired to delay his trip. Vital telephone calls had come in late, and then had been prolonged by poor connections, inexplicable interruptions. These had caused him to be late in arriving for his conference with President Andrew Warren, where he was kept waiting while the Chief Executive freed himself from an avalanche of last-minute demands on his attention. Finally, Jimmy's car had refused to perform properly. The motor had sputtered and missed so badly that he had switched to another machine—only to have *it* develop a slow-leak flat tire when he was nearly a mile from the nearest garage.

Petty annoyances, perhaps—and yet it was significant that they had all combined to detain him on this very day when he was so determined to get to Philadelphia in time for the mammoth American Peace Rally scheduled there this evening. American Peace Rally.... Jimmy's eyes smoldered and his lean jaw squared belligerently as that fine-sounding phrase flashed through his troubled mind. Fine-sounding, but possibly deceptive!

The American Peace Rally was to be a demonstration staged by the nation's pacifist organizations, under the leadership of Professor Seymour Durant's Legion of Noncombatants. In their zeal for peace these misguided idealists would strip America of her arms, leaving her unprotected and helpless in a world now infested with brigand nations—each covetously eyeing the wealth and territory of its neighbors. This meeting tonight was to be the climax of their drive against the vital army and navy appropriation bill now before Congress—a demonstration calculated to intimidate legislators into closing the pursestrings and strangling the defenses upon which America's very existence depended!

Misguided idealists.... It seemed impossible that thinking men could be so short-sighted, so criminally blind. Jimmy wondered whether there was not more to this rear-guard onslaught than appeared on the surface; whether the motives behind it were actually entirely idealistic. Several times during the past few weeks his undercover aides had brought him rumors of a *coup* of some sort which was to be sprung at the rally.

"They're waiting for it all through the country, Operator 5," Ben Hatcher had warned from Chicago. "I've picked up an inkling of it here, and Lloyd Martin has detected it in Minneapolis. Seems as if they are just waiting for a signal."

What that *coup* was to be, Jimmy had no idea—but he intended to find out. That was why it was so imperative that he be at the meeting—that he reach the big Municipal Conven-

tion Hall before the pacifist spellbinders succeeded in doing real harm to the country....

At last he was speeding through the outskirts of Philadelphia approaching the business section. Fretfully he glanced at the clock and then back at the long canyon of the street ahead. It was clearly revealed by the glowing sky above it.

Jimmy Christopher looked at that sky more closely. Tonight there seemed more than the usual evening glow that reflected from thousands of electric signs. The sky was more red than he had ever seen it—a flaming crimson. As he stared at it, the light seemed to pulsate, to waver and leap like the illumination from a huge bonfire!

A CURIOUS apprehension crept over the man whom America knew best as Operator 5. His foot jammed down harder on the accelerator. Yet before he had gone two blocks more he was tied up in a traffic jam. For some minutes he had noticed that the traffic approaching him from the center of town was unusually heavy. Now it became a veritable deluge—a steady stream of cars that rushed toward him at top speed, crowding one another and usurping the entire roadway.

Vainly Jimmy pressed down on his siren. The cars ahead were jammed as tightly as his own—as tightly as those that were now closing in behind him. Sirens were screaming, but their plaint was useless. The din made no impression on the drivers of those on-coming cars, now pressing so close that they actually rubbed running-boards and fenders with the machines they were crowding off the road.

Jimmy caught a fleeting glimpse of the faces of several of those drivers—the faces of men who crouched over their wheels in utter terror! Wild-eyed, panic-stricken faces! The faces of men who seemed to have but one thought—to flee; to get away, no matter how!

Then he heard the sound he had felt was inevitable—a loud crash, the rending of steel, shattering of glass. A collision! Instantly it was followed by others. In a few moments dozens of cars were piled up inextricably—a twisted mass of wreckage that completely blocked the street from curb to curb.

Out of those stalled cars now poured hundreds of terror-maddened passengers—screaming women, wailing children, cursing men. They climbed out of doors and windows; vied with one another in clambering over the tightly packed cars, their frightened eyes probing wildly for a way of escape.

"Fire!" Jimmy heard them scream. "Fire! Fire!"

In the midst of the frantic turmoil he saw an old woman go down; saw her roll in the street. But she was back on her knees before he could reach her side. There on the edge of the sidewalk she knelt, her hands clasped in prayer, begging the Almighty for mercy and succor from the flames. Just in time he snatched her up, saving her from being trodden underfoot by the oncoming mob.

"You're all right!" he shouted, "Don't worry—I'll get you out of this!"

She did not seem to hear him; did not seem to be aware that he was there beside her. A babble of prayer flowed ceaselessly, tonelessly, from her lips—a babble out of which he could catch only phrases.

"—end of the world…. Day of Judgment… whole world on fire… punishment for sins…." Disjointed phrases in the eerie, inhuman voice of the insane. He looked into her eyes and saw that all understanding had fled from them. She was utterly mad, her mind shattered by terror!

Jimmy managed to lead her to the end of the constantly growing tangle of cars. There he left her and joined the fleeing crowd, raced with them until he reached a subway entrance. But even as he reached the head of the steps he knew his intention was useless. Up from the lower level came the roar of sheer bedlam. The shrill blast of train whistles, the terrified screaming of women, the frenzied cursing of men—all blended into a thunderous paean of horror. People were fighting their way up desperately from below, while others battled just as frantically to get down to the platform. The tracks were jammed with stalled trains.

In the space of a few minutes all of Philadelphia seemed to have become a madhouse. Traffic was at a standstill, and the streets swarmed with wild-eyed people who ran as if Death was reaching out to grab them at every step. Ran until they could run no longer; until they leaned exhausted against the buildings or sank to the sidewalk.

"What is it? What's the matter?" Jimmy demanded, as he grabbed hold of a man who could barely stand on his feet. "What happened? What's going on back there?"

"Fire!" the fellow panted, as he gasped for breath. "Fire—everywhere! Broad Street—all on fire—buildings—street—people! Red monsters—spreading fire everywhere!"

Monsters spreading fire…. These people were mad, all of them! Jimmy turned from the fellow and dived into the crowd. Grimly he fought his way through them, but now the worst of the rush was over. The crowd was thinning yet the faces he glimpsed were even worse than before; faces of men and women who looked as if they had just stepped from hell itself!

Jimmy ignored the warnings they shouted at him. Past them he ran, until he reached the forward end of that glut of immovable cars. There he spied a policeman's motorcycle nosed into the jam and abandoned by its rider. Quickly he backed it, got it clear of the tangle and vaulted into the seat. In a moment he had it up on the sidewalk, siren screaming, headed in the direction of that glowing sky!

QUICKLY HE was past the fleeing crowd—past all but moaning stragglers who crept along on hands and knees, charred corpses that lay smoldering in the street! Jimmy stared at those horrible, blackened forms with popping eyes—and then he turned a corner. The end of the street was livid with flames! Flames that were creeping down the side street from the avenue—from the inferno that was Broad Street!

In a moment he had reached the center of the conflagration. Aghast, he stopped at the wide thoroughfare that was the heart of Philadelphia. Now it was a huge furnace, from side to side. Wherever he looked, everything seemed to be burning—buildings, telephone poles, corpses that littered the sidewalks. That fire was consuming everything! Everything but an amazing object that stood out there in the center of the street....

Jimmy gaped at that astounding apparition with incredulous eyes and was overwhelmed by the feeling that this all must be a weird nightmare; that he would wake up and find that he had been dreaming. That fantastic object was some kind of aircraft—

the most gigantic he had ever seen! A curiously streamlined air-cruiser that dwarfed the largest Zeppelin the world had ever known! An enormous airship that was blocks long—and that was studded with doors and runways that led from them like the gangplanks of an ocean liner!

Again he batted his eyes unbelievingly—and then he knew what that panting fugitive had meant about monsters running around in the flames. There *were* monsters—hundreds of them! Monsters from some other impossible world! Creatures that wore tight-fitting red outfits that covered them from their feet to the enormous globes that served them for heads! Grotesque creatures that could not be of this world. Back through the doors of their incredible ship they were swarming, dragging with them helpless women captives!

Frantically the half-denuded women screamed for help. But their pleas fell upon deaf ears—until Jimmy Christopher bent low over the bars of his motorcycle and headed straight for that demon-ship! The moment he swung into Broad Street it was as if he were riding through the door of an oven—or the entrance to hell. Waves of heat beat down upon him from every side— from the windows and doorways of the burning buildings, from the flaming fronts of solid brick and stone!

Those brick and stone walls were burning as if they were no more than the driest tinder! Fire that could consume bricks and stone and solid steel—that was preposterous! Yet, there it was before his smarting, heat-seared eyes! There those solid, unburnable materials were being consumed as if they were no more than false-front movie props....

It was all unreal, impossible—all except the roar and heat of those devouring flames. The darting tongues licked out hungrily at the speeding motorcycle, but it flashed past each threatening trap—until suddenly a metal light-pole that was blazing like a shaft of dried pine buckled in the middle and toppled to the ground.

Too late Jimmy saw it going down. Desperately he tried to steer clear, but there was no time. The blazing pole dropped directly in front of him—and then the motorcycle was right on top of it, plowing into it, bucking over it crazily, veering sharply to one side and toppling over, to spill him headlong.

Even the pavement was hot as he sprawled upon it. But he was up again in an instant, scrambling to his feet and diving to one side just in time to avoid the charge of one of those weird-looking creatures who was coming at him out of the flames. Under one arm the monster clutched a curious-looking apparatus that seemed to be some sort of projector. He pressed a lever at its side, there was the flash of an electric contact—and Jimmy's coat suddenly took fire!

The flames spread as if they were feeding on excelsior, but before they could reach his face Jimmy spied a means of salvation. A fountain stood no more than twenty feet away. Instantly he sprinted to it and flung himself into the water, submerged his body until the blaze was extinguished.

The water in that fountain was hot; so hot that it seemed on the verge of boiling. Then he realized why. *The fountain itself was on fire!* Flames danced around the stone rim and enveloped the metal figure in the center that held up four cornucopias from which the water poured. An amazing mingling of fire and water—with the hot streams spurting from flaming funnels!

Surely a madhouse phenomenon of that sort could happen only in a fantastic nightmare! But there was no doubting the reality of that hot water. Nor was there any doubt about that strange-looking creature who came loping toward the fountain, the projector trained down on the water that covered all but Jimmy's head.

The dancing light of the flames played on the fellow's tight-fitting red costume; made it look as if it were part of his body—a rubbery hide beneath a great round dome of a head. That huge globular cranium was featureless except for two round eyes that stared from it like the lenses of binoculars. Jimmy stared at the weird-looking creature—and recalled imaginative drawings of the supposed inhabitants of Mars that might have been its brothers!

Martians invading the earth! Now he knew that he must be on the verge of insanity!

But that incredible flame-walker was bearing down upon him, and Jimmy dared not stir from his watery haven. Instinct told him that he would die, that he would be burned to a crisp, the moment his body was exposed to the ray of the projector that had set him on fire. The water was his only refuge. But even that would be useless once the creature reached him, for now Jimmy saw that he clutched a pistol as well as the projector.

Grimly he drew his own automatic from its sodden holster, although he was already convinced that it would be useless. Even if the water did not jam it, something told him that its bullets would have no effect on that red, hide-like covering—no more effect than peas shot at the hide of a rhinoceros. The gun was a futile thing. This was the end. In another moment the murderous creature would be upon him—

But at that moment a shrill blast sounded clear above the roar of the flames—a blast that stabbed into Jimmy's ears like the blade of a knife. Instantly the oncoming creature whirled and started back to the ship. When Jimmy raised his head above the surface of the hot water he saw that all of the despoilers were doing likewise. Crouched there in the fountain, he watched them file through the doors, watched the runways drawn up and the doors closed. In little more than a minute it was finished, and then the great ship seemed to explode!

Blasts of flame shot out of one end with a roar that was deafening, and in the same moment the air-monster streaked off into the darkness. A rocket-ship! That explained its lack of wings, its peculiar streamlined construction—a rocket-ship that had come out of the sky and now was returning there, taking scores of women captives with it....

NOW THAT it was gone, the whole experience seemed even more wildly improbable than before. Jimmy stared at the empty street where the gigantic invader had so recently stood. Surely, he must have imagined that scene. Perhaps it had been a sort of mirage, a trick of the dancing flames.

But those flaming buildings were no nightmare. That burning stone was actuality, no matter how impossible its present state might seem. Into the hot water beside him dropped a flaming chunk of the fountain, and Jimmy climbed over the flame-girt edge, to stand staring at the conflagration, while an eerie chill trickled down his spine.

Death and destruction were nothing new to Operator 5. He had seen America laid waste from coast to coast, had seen the country ground under the heel of a foreign despot when the conquering hordes of the Purple Empire had overrun it. He had faced the weapons of barbarians and the latest of modern scientific death-contrivances. Yet nothing had given him quite the strange, unreal feeling of that sinister space-ship with its supernatural-looking crew. Nothing had affected him quite so profoundly as that unholy fire which now consumed objects which should have been *unconsumable!*

Resolutely he shook off the near-coma that had held him transfixed. The fire was spreading. It would sweep the entire city unless it was gotten under control. Now he saw that he was not entirely alone with the burning corpses that littered the street in every direction. Dazed men and women were beginning to dart from the flame-wrapped doorways of hotels. Some of the more daring of those who had fled were returning, were peering into Broad Street from around corners, to see what was happening now that the deadly invader was gone.

Jimmy Christopher raced to the nearest group.

"The danger is over!" He shouted his reassurance as they turned and started to run from him. "They're gone—but there are men and women here who need help. This fire must be stopped before it spreads farther. I need help from all of you now!"

Gradually he penetrated their panic, forced them to understand. A police sergeant led the way and the sight of him seemed to inspire confidence in the others. Jimmy delegated several to go after fire apparatus. The others he divided into squads and assigned them to sections of the street, to aid the wounded and rescue those who still could be saved from the blazing buildings.

It was a ghastly task. Picking his way between the crisped bodies that lay scattered everywhere, Operator 5 stared down with narrowed eyes at corpses that blazed as if they were made of oil and pitch instead of flesh and blood. Once the flames reached a victim he was doomed. No amount of effort could check the blaze from eating its way fiercely into the bodies. However there were scores of hysterical women and utterly demoralized men who had not yet been reached by the deadly flame tongues. They could still be saved, unless....

At that moment Jimmy saw a man stagger blindly through a blazing doorway; saw a burning ember drop down and touch the doomed man's shoulder—and instantly his whole body was wrapped in flames!

These doomed ones could be saved, unless they came in contact with the flames. Jimmy shuddered involuntarily, as he realized how closely death hovered all around him. His soaked clothing had been some protection, but now it was drying, steaming. If one of those flame tongues reached out and touched him now he would perish horribly, like that screaming, writhing victim....

But the work of rescue *must* go on!

At last the re-awakened fire companies arrived, and the space where the rocket-ship had stood was now filled with fire-fighting apparatus. There was little to be done that would save the blazing buildings. Once that consuming fire claimed them, it seemed to eat its way deeper and deeper—inevitable.... Those buildings were doomed. However, by concentrating on others that stood in the path of the flames the firemen gradually brought the holocaust under control.

For hours Jimmy Christopher was everywhere in that devastating area, leading the rescue work, helping the still shaky firemen, giving his aid wherever needed. And as he worked his brain was whirling at top speed, trying to grasp the real significance of this catastrophe; endeavoring to fathom the identity of those incredible invaders.

It was obviously impossible that they were Martians. But from where else could they have come? America was at peace with the world. Operator 5's thoughts turned back to the American Peace Rally for which he had been bound. Was it possible that those misguided fanatics could have had anything to do with this fearful outrage? Was it possible that this could be the *coup* about which his men had heard those vague yet ominous rumors?

That was as wildly improbable as the Martian theory. Jimmy dismissed the idea. But now a fresh worry obsessed him. The

Municipal Convention Hall had stood right there on Broad Street. All that remained of the big building was a roaring bonfire that soared upward through the chimney of four partly crumbled walls. The American Peace Rally was over, but what had become of its huge audience?

Among that doomed audience had been a freckle-faced, pug-nosed young fellow who was one of Jimmy's most trusted assistants—one of that little group that had stood so steadfastly by his side through America's darkest hours. Tim Donovan had been more than an assistant to Operator 5; more even than a brother. A waif of the New York streets, he had come into Jimmy Christopher's life one dark night, years ago, when the warning he shouted from the hallway in which he crouched had saved Jimmy from a criminal's bullet.

After that Jimmy had taken the wiry little bootblack under his wing and soon discovered that Tim possessed many sterling qualities. Between them had developed a remarkable trust, devotion and admiration. Operator 5 became Tim's ideal, his idol, the leader whose orders he followed implicitly and for whom he gladly would have laid down his life…. Tim, attuned to America's best interests, had attended that peace rally with three companions of his own age—three youths whom he had enlisted in what Operator 5 had jocularly termed his Junior Auxiliary. They must have been there when that space-ship swooped down into Broad Street—but where were they now?

Involuntarily Jimmy's eyes darted to the mounds of charred corpses that were piled in front of the building. His heart

15

constricted. Was Tim somewhere in that ghastly pile, his young life sacrificed at last on the altar of his fervid patriotism?

Even to search through those grisly mounds would not answer that question, for those poor corpses were changed beyond recognition. Jimmy turned away and threw himself with renewed vigor into the tasks that surrounded him on every side.

At last the blaze was conquered. But the gutted buildings were reduced to piles of smoldering embers and the corpses of the victims had been gathered into improvised morgues now besieged by thousands of grieving relatives. Jimmy's eyes were hard and his jaws clenched tightly as he gazed at those scenes of misery and suffering. But the damage of that night, he knew, would be far greater than the actual destruction of life and property.

This would be only the beginning. From it would spread a terror that probably would soon be nationwide....

Even before he managed to extricate his car from the traffic jam, he realized that his fears were justified. All around him he heard auto radios screaming the news of the disaster, broadcasting it to the four corners of listening America.

"The United States has been invaded by men from another world!" one excited announcer shouted. "A great spaceship, of tremendous size, landed in the center of Philadelphia shortly after eight o'clock this evening. It disgorged a savage band of weird-looking creatures who spread fire and death all around them. The heart of Philadelphia has been reduced to fire-blasted ruin in which thousands of citizens perished.

"From descriptions furnished by some of the survivors, these

barbarous invaders have been identi-
fied as inhabitants of the planet Mars.
Armed with a strange fire that consumes
even stone and steel, they were irresistible. No man could stand against them,
and not one of them lost his life in the
ten minutes of hell that transformed
the Quaker City's Broad Street into a
shambles!"

It went on....

"The poor fool," Jimmy Christopher groaned inwardly. The
announcer was simply setting the torch to a panic that would
sweep the nation from coast to coast!

If only he had waited; if only he could have been gagged
until a sane story of the onslaught was given to the nation....
But now that was too late. The damage had been done—by this
announcer and a dozen others.

"The space-ship disappeared as swiftly as it came." The
excited voice was merely adding fuel to the mounting flame
of terror it had kindled. "It may reappear again at any time—
anywhere. All citizens are warned to keep off the streets and
stay in their homes. All municipalities are urged to organize
watchers and institute a system of alarms. Further bulletins will
be broadcast the moment measures have been taken to combat
this terrifying doom that has descended upon us from nowhere."

Into every city and county that voice and others like it were
going; and in their wake was sure to follow a shuddering terror

that would spread like wildfire and leave America stunned and panic-stricken!

CHAPTER 2
KINDLING FIRES

TIM DONOVAN'S gray-blue eyes were steely. His face was unusually white beneath the thickly strewn freckles as he sat in Philadelphia's Municipal Convention Hall and listened… listened to heresy, distorted truth and thinly coated lies that made his blood boil. That great hall was packed with nearly thirty thousand spectators—poor, misguided fools who were unconsciously conspiring to betray their country and turn her out, defenseless, to face the wolves that yapped at her doors.

Up there on the speakers' platform were the pacifist orators and leaders of the American Peace Rally—men whose blindness seemed incredible to Tim. Some of them, he knew, had seen war and therefore should know what it meant. Some had served in the dark days of the Purple Invasion—days when only the indomitable spirit of Operator 5 stood between America and the abject slavery that would have swiftly followed in the wake of surrender. But others—theorists, idealists—merely contemplated the national problem from the security of their sheltered university libraries.

Professor Seymour Durant—the thin, scholarly chairman, with his mane of gray-white hair that was reminiscent of Henry Ward Beecher—knew nothing of war and the avarice of nations. He was a philosopher who had unaccountably been swept up by the tide of pacifist sentiment and pushed to its crest as president of the League of Noncombatants. His poet's features became eloquent with indignation when he spoke of war, but that was all he knew about it....

It was likewise with a dozen more of those distinguished-looking savants who sat beside Durant. They were the front for the pacifist movement, but they were ill-equipped to cope with the problems of war and national defense. As Tim looked at them, he felt again that they were little more than puppets. It was the others who pulled the strings and motivated this dangerous movement now spreading so alarmingly.

The dangerous ones were men like Myron Sumner, vice-president of the league, who was now addressing the assemblage. Sumner was a fighter; husky, broad-shouldered, thirty-five, he had seen active service during the Purple Invasion. A soldier, he knew of what he spoke. In consequence, now, in Tim Donovan's eyes, he was a despicable traitor.

"Millions of dollars for guns and battleships! Millions of dollars for tanks and armored planes! Millions of dollars for high explosives and deadly poison gas!" Sumner's vibrant voice rang through the quiet hall. "Millions of dollars to kill other people, while our own citizens are in want and in misery—while many of them are starving to death! These millions of dollars are wasted, when they are so badly needed.

"Why? They are poured into the greedy coffers of the merchants of murder, the ammunition-makers, the armament-builders! Millions of dollars for these leeches who have fastened themselves on the national administration and are sucking the United States Treasury dry!"

Now the hall was no longer silent. The hushed quiet had given way to a rumble of indignation. Men were shouting approval of Sumner's speech. Women were standing up and cheering wildly. Myron Sumner's dark eyes flashed with satisfaction, his broad, square face flushed with triumph. He held these listeners now— in the palm of his hand, ready to follow his dictates.

"The dingo leeches are hungry again!" he thundered. "They are waiting for a new gorging. This week a docile Congress will listen to the voices of its masters and betray you and every other American citizen by passing the annual raid on the Treasury that is called the Army and Navy Appropriations Bill! I say this disgraceful steal, this outrageous squandering of the public funds, will be perpetrated again this week—*unless* you stand up and stop it!"

Tim Donovan listened to no more. Hot rage flooded his brain and his hands balled into hard fists as he leaped to his feet.

"That's a deliberate lie—and you know it!" he shouted, as he reached the aisle and charged toward the platform. "Every contract under the Appropriations Bill will be open to public bidding. Every item has been debated for months and whittled down to the lowest safe figure. To defeat this bill would be to stab America in the back!"

His voice was drowned, his words lost in the bedlam that arose from every part of the hall. But now he had reached the platform, was springing up the steps, intent on confronting Sumner before that vast audience and hurling his lies into his teeth. Men rose and tried to stop him, endeavored to push him back. But Tim brushed past them. He gained the floor of the platform where Sumner met him.

Sumner's face twisted into a bleak mask of rage. He sprang forward and swung his fist savagely at Tim's head—but the blow missed its mark. Tim had danced back out of the way—only to leap in swiftly and snap an uppercut to Sumner's jaw. The hot blood was pounding in Tim's veins. He tingled with satisfaction. This snarling liar was as base a traitor as ever had tried to betray America, and a traitor was one creature that Tim Donovan could not abide....

Grimly he followed up his advantage. He stepped in closer and flailed his fists into Sumner's face, drove him back and then lifted him from his feet. Myron Sumner went down, but he was back on his feet again in an instant. Now he gripped an automatic whipped from his hip pocket. That automatic was pointed at Tim's heart.

Stark murder was in Sumner's eyes at that moment. In his savage rage he had forgotten where he was, what he was doing. Everything was forgotten except the frenzied desire to kill this fellow who had struck and floored him in the sight of all these thousands. Sumner's finger pressed back on the trigger. But the instant the weapon roared his arm was seized, pulled back.

"No! No, Myron—you mustn't!" a girl screamed, as the bullet embedded itself harmlessly in the high ceiling....

FOR THE split-second of that swift action, Tim Donovan had stood there immobile, helpless to move a muscle as he steeled himself for the smashing impact of the bullet that would

21

mean his death. It was Maureen Durant who saved him—Maureen, the pert-faced, auburn-haired daughter of Professor Durant. Her five-foot figure was dwarfed as she clung to Sumner. But her hands fastened onto his arm and gripped it desperately until others on the platform sprang to her aid and twisted the weapon from Sumner's fingers.

Myron Sumner's face was apoplectic. Rage that muted his tongue flashed from his eyes. In that moment, Tim realized, the man was utterly mad.

Maureen Durant appeared to realize it, too. Her hazel eyes were wide with fear, her pretty face blanched. Desperately she clung to Sumner—and for an instant it seemed that he would sweep her aside, hurl her down into the audience.

By now the vast hall was in an uproar. Men and women were on their feet, shouting and yelling as they surged toward the platform.

"Throw him out! Lynch him! Kill him!" they screamed as they fought to get within reach of Tim. "Kill the spy!"

From the corner of his eye, Tim saw his friends battling with the infuriated mob; saw two of them go down, another grimly fighting off those who would climb up onto the platform. Four of them against nearly ten times as many thousands! They would be overwhelmed, torn to pieces....

But suddenly there was a terrific crash somewhere outside the hall; a crash that thundered above the wild pandemonium and then silenced it, miraculously. Wondering, half-frightened, men and women paused and stared questioningly at one another in the moment of strange silence that followed. Then, as one, they seemed to *smell* their danger.

Fire! The tang of smoke! A wisp of it was curling in from the direction of the entrance, hanging like a portent of doom over their heads! Fire!

The panicky word was on thousands of lips, half-uttered, when a stentorian voice shouted the alarm that already gripped them.

"Run for your lives!" it bellowed. "The whole city is on fire!"

Like frightened cattle they stampeded from the great auditorium, knocking one another down as they crowded into the aisles and fought to reach the corridors and exits. Already disorganized by the uproar the sound of Sumner's gun had precipitated, they lost all restraint as that ominous wisp of smoke grew thicker and spread out in a heavy, acrid cloud.

Hundreds were trampled to death in that mad struggle. But at last the doors of the building were thrown wide. The terrified pacifists poured out into the street, only to stand there stunned, gaping in horror at a world that seemed to be in flames all around them! A world that was dominated by a huge, strange-looking airship from which hundreds of demonlike figures were deploying, leaping through the flames of hell....

THE WILD panic that swept that hall was not confined to the audience. In a few moments the several dozen speakers and officials on the platform were down among the others, battling their way to the nearest doorway and the safety it promised. Tim Donovan was alone, forgotten, as he stood looking out over that frenzied riot.

What had happened, he did not know—but what was happening in those close-packed aisles he could see all too plainly. Those apostles of peace had suddenly become wild animals, ready to use tooth and nail—any weapon that came to hand—in their frenzied battle for life. Age or sex meant nothing to them. Women were only to be pushed aside as the stronger males surged past them.

Tim's eyes widened. That blue-clad figure who was struggling helplessly in the milling pack was Maureen Durant. Tim saw her frightened face turned upward appealingly, saw her go down—and then he leaped down from the platform and went to her rescue. She was leaning against a seat, barely able to stand, when he gained her side and drew her back to a place of temporary safety.

"Take it easy," he warned. "We have time. There isn't any sign of fire yet—and a sure way to be killed is to allow that frightened mob to trample over you."

"I know," she gasped. "I tried to follow my father and my brother—but they were swallowed up by the crowd."

Tim took charge of her. Patiently he waited until most of the crowd had fought their way out of the auditorium. Then he retraced his steps to the speaker's platform and explored the section behind it. As he expected, there was a corridor in the rear. It led to an exit that had not even been opened.

Tim pulled the bolt, pushed the door wide—and stepped out into a blazing inferno! The whole side of the building above his head was in flames—and so was every building that he could see on both sides of the street! Flames everywhere, converting

24

Broad Street into a raging furnace in which terrified thousands ran blindly!

Among those panic-stricken victims stalked grotesque-looking creatures that looked like huge-headed monsters! Only then did Tim spy the great ship from which they had come—and from which their fellows were still pouring in a steady stream. Hundreds of them, armed with peculiar mechanical contraptions with wide, round muzzles that were now turned on the crowd.

Tim caught the white spark as those strange weapons went into action—and then, before his eyes, the screaming victims burst into flames! Men and women, burning as if they were made of straw!

Flames that roared through the crowd like a grass-fire racing through a stand of dry stubble. Everything went down before them; everything was swallowed up, became additional fuel to feed the mounting blaze!

That much Tim Donovan saw at once. Then he realized his own danger—and was quick to meet it. Grabbing Maureen Durant by the arm, he yanked her back inside the door and slammed it shut behind them.

"Oh, God!" she moaned. "What is happening out there? What—"

Her voice trailed off into a horrified silence. She did not expect Tim to answer that question. The words had been automatic, a subconscious reaction to the ghastly scene she had witnessed.

Tim Donovan had no idea what had happened—but he did

know that death had been very close to them as they cowered there in the doorway. His nostrils still tingled with the peculiar odor he had sniffed in the air; the fresh, crisp odor of oxygen. Just for an instant he had caught it—and then he had dived to the protection of the corridor.

How long they could stay there he had no way of telling. Smoke was creeping in at the sides of the door now, and the crackle of flames was like the rattle of a machine-gun as the building blazed above them. Back into the auditorium he led the way. But now he could hardly see across the hall. Great clouds of smoke billowed into it; smoke that seemed to seek them out and reach clutching fingers for their throats.

"Cover your nose!" he panted the warning, as he took the girl by the hand and ran through the gray blanket to a doorway at the farther end of the building.

Perhaps there the flames would not yet have reached. Possibly they would be able to slip out and gain the protection of a side street before the blaze engulfed them. Staggering, gasping for breath, they reached the exit and climbed over the bodies now piled behind it. Outside, the way seemed clear—and when Tim stepped into the street he saw the reason for that desolation. Sprawled on the sidewalk and in the gutter were hundreds of corpses... hundreds of inert bodies that blazed furiously!

And through the flames stalked those monstrous red destroyers!

Hundreds of them—and one of them was right there on top of them! A red-covered creature with a huge head that was like an inverted fish-bowl! Out of the flames this fiend stepped and leaped forward with surprising ease, to grasp Maureen by the wrist and drag her after him!

Tim saw the girl struggle, and go down. The weird creature leaped upon her and seized her in its arms. Her terrified scream rang out shrilly—shocking Tim out of the coma of helplessness that had momentarily engulfed him. From his pocket he drew the automatic Myron Sumner had dropped on the platform. He aimed it at that crimson devil, pressed the trigger… but the shot seemed to have no effect.

Again and again Tim fired, aiming at the monster's body and great round head. But the bullets were ineffective. That loose crimson hide and the globular head were made of something that was impenetrable….

Maureen saw what had happened and read in it her doom. The realization of her utter helplessness drove her frantic. Wildly she fought her captor, beat her fists against his great headpiece as she struggled to slip from his grasp. And then Tim was at her side, using his automatic as a club to smash against that massive head.

Twice his blows landed, but they had no effect whatever. His fingers tingled from the impact, but the automatic barrel did not even dent the strange helmet. Again he smashed down at it with all his strength—but before he could strike the creature's heavy fist whipped out and landed against the side of his head with the force of a pile driver.

All the world seemed to explode in front of Tim's eyes. The red glare of the blaze turned to a blinding white. The roaring of the flames increased until the noise filled his whole skull—but above that din he knew that he heard a sharp, piercing whistle that seemed to reach down into his drowning consciousness.

That whistle.... The red devil-creature.... He had whirled—was running back toward the fantastic airship.... And then Tim Donovan's eyes closed and he knew no more....

MAUREEN DURANT had been quick to take advantage of the momentary diversion of Tim's desperate attack and finally had managed to tear herself free from her monstrous captor. She was free for a split-second, and then the creature again lunged for her—but before it could recapture her that deafening whistle split the air and brought it up short.

Instantly the creature whirled, seemed to lose all interest in her. Straight back toward the ship it darted, to be joined by others who came running from every direction. Into the many doors they swarmed—and before the girl had time to realize the fact of her deliverance the great airliner roared off into the night and disappeared as completely as if it had never existed.

Maureen had escaped. But those diabolical creatures might return at any moment and recapture her! Panic took hold of her, but she remembered Tim Donovan. He lay there helpless in the street, directly in the path of the fear-crazed survivors who now came running blindly from the doorways of those blazing buildings.

She could not leave him there like that!

Swiftly she bent over, gripped Tim under the shoulders. He was too heavy for her to lift, but she could drag him. At least she could get him out of the way to a place of comparative safety.

Down a side street she pulled him. It was the side street on which her father had parked his car.

Was the car still there where he had left it? What had happened to him and her brother? Were they alive, or had they perished in those awful flames?

Those questions were answered even before she reached the car. Half-way down the block her brother, Gerald Durant, met her and quickly stooped to relieve her of her burden. Together they carried Tim to the car where Professor Durant sat, refusing to think of his own safety until his daughter had been found.

With Gerald at the wheel, the car headed away from the flaming horror that, a few minutes before, had been Philadelphia's proudest thoroughfare. Too overcome for words by the appalling sights they had witnessed, the Durants sat silently peering out at the panic-stricken city as the sedan sped toward the west.

It was then that Tim Donovan came back to consciousness....
That was Maureen beside him in the back seat, he recognized; and in a flash of illumination from an arc-light he recognized Seymour Durant beside the driver. Now the car was nearing the outskirts of the city, was pressing steadily westward in the direction of Overlook Hills. Tim lay back on the cushion and watched as the car glided through the fashionable suburb, finally turned in at a large estate. It was carefully guarded, he noted. Hidden watchers at the entrance stepped out to intercept them and exchange a few words with the driver.

Tim's nerves tingled. This was not merely a residence; it was a stronghold for the pacifist plotters! Yes, there were others already at hand. Nearly a dozen cars were drawn up beside the big stone building, and several men came out to meet them the moment the car halted. They opened the door and peered inside suspiciously as they helped Maureen out.

Tim groaned and held his hands to his bowed head. Dazedly he accepted the aid of the hands that reached in to help him; stumbled out and would have fallen to the ground if they had not caught him. Dizzily he swayed there, half-slumped in their arms.

"Take him inside quickly," Maureen urged. "He is sick—badly hurt. Can't you see that he can hardly stand?"

Doubtfully they started to obey, but at that moment another car swung into the drive; and out hopped Myron Sumner. Straight to the Durant car he came running—to stop directly in their path and glare at Tim with eyes that snapped out of a hard, set face.

"Why did you bring him here?" he swung on Maureen. "You know who he is, don't you? Clemons and Artley recognized him. He is Tim Donovan—one of Operator 5's pet snoopers. Perhaps you think it was a mere accident that he was in the hall tonight when our meeting was broken up by that murderous raid? And now you bring him here!"

Hostile suspicion flared in his dark eyes—suspicion and something more. Tim watched him closely and recognized what it was. Jealousy. Myron Sumner was jealous of the concern Maureen was showing for another man. But she overruled him.

"I don't know anything about that, Myron," the girl said calmly, firmly. "I only know that he is badly hurt—because he

30

INVASION FROM THE SKY

JIMMY CHRISTOPHER

tried to defend me. He is coming inside with us and is going to stay here until he recovers."

Sumner did not reply. He stepped back and let them pass. Into the house they led Tim, and then upstairs to a small bedroom on the second floor. A butler came at Maureen's call and took charge of him; put him to bed and volunteered to do anything to make him comfortable.

"Sleep—that's all I need," Tim muttered, as he turned over on the pillow and closed his eyes.

The butler softly left the room, and the big house was silent… for a few moments. Then Tim caught the sound of cautious footsteps in the hall, heard a key turn almost noiselessly in the lock. As quietly as they had approached, the footsteps receded.

For long minutes Tim lay there, listening intently. Then he got out of bed, all evidence of his pretended weakness vanished, and padded softly to the door. It was locked, and the key had been removed. Quickly he got into his clothes and took a key-ring from his trousers pocket. Two of the keys on that ring were designed to open a myriad of locks. They made short work of the old-fashioned one before him.

The corridor was deserted when he stepped out into it. The upper floor was quiet, but he caught the rumble of many voices coming from below. Some sort of meeting was going on down there.

SWIFTLY TIM reconnoitered that upper floor and found a stairway in the rear. He encountered nobody as he went down, and flitted through the lower hallway like a shadow—guided by the sound of those voices. They led him to a large drawing-room in the center of the building. He was able to approach it from the rear, and flatten himself against the wall behind a drapery-hung doorway.

There were nearly fifty men in that room. Gathered in a circle around a large table, they were listening to Myron Sumner, who stood thumping the table-top with a clenched fist.

"That was no accident!" he snorted. "I suppose you will tell me those murdering devils came from Mars or from the moon! I'll tell you where they came from—Washington, D.C.! Andy Warren is licked, and he knows it. We have sufficient votes to defeat his army and navy bill. He was desperate—and that melodramatic raid was his answer to us. Operator 5 had his spies there in the hall to break up our meeting—and in the midst of the uproar that hell broke loose outside. Perfectly timed!"

"That seems to be going too far, Myron," Seymour Durant protested mildly. "Surely neither the President nor Operator 5 would countenance wholesale murder and destruction—"

But Sumner swept his objection aside, brusquely.

" 'For the good of the nation' they will do anything," he snapped. "With the nation panic-stricken by this bizarre attack, Congress will fall all over itself passing the appropriation bill—or so they think. But we are going to have something more to say about that! We have tried to attain our objectives by peaceful means. That has failed. Now we have no choice but to fight them with their own weapons."

His eyes swept the gathering, flashing significantly as they flashed from face to face. Then Myron Sumner dropped all

pretense and stepped out in the
role he had been rehearsing for
months.

"We feared something of
this sort—and we prepared for
it," he clipped. "Our organization is ready in all the principal cities of the nation, waiting
for the word to go into action.
Tomorrow I will give that
word. We can't wait any longer.
If the appropriation bill passes,

all our work will be undone—but *before* it can pass we will be in
complete control of the government!"

There it was—the hidden motive behind these pacifist activi-
ties that Operator 5 had suspected! Boldly Myron Sumner stood
there and faced them, the confessed leader of an organization
that had been deliberately weakening the national defense so
that it could seize control of the government! An outfit of plotters who had been driven out into the open by that murderous
raid they attributed to the federal authorities!

For a moment there was quiet. Then the room was in an
uproar. Seymour Durant was on his feet, his face white, demanding attention.

"I know nothing about this," he shouted above the uproar.
"This is sedition—treacherous plotting!"

But they howled him down. Myron Sumner nodded his head,
and Durant was seized with a dozen of his companions. Now

there was no more need for the "front" those distinguished oldsters had afforded. Now Sumner brushed them aside and took complete charge himself. Durant and the others were bustled from the room, and Sumner and his aides went into executive session.

This was the reason for those guards at the entrance to the estate, Tim realized. This was to be Sumner's headquarters, the stronghold from which he would direct the rebellion that would overthrow the government. Now the men who had led Durant and the genuine pacifists from the room were returning, their faces grinning with elation. The prisoners, Tim gathered, had been confined in rooms long held ready for them.

Tim tensed. Two of Sumner's men were returning by way of the corridor behind him! He was trapped—bound to be discovered when they reached the doorway! And this time Maureen Durant would not be there to save his life when Myron Sumner leaped at him!

Tim's mind worked swiftly. He could not wait there to be discovered and seized. There was only one alternative—and he grabbed it. Leaping from behind the curtain, he crouched low and dashed down the corridor—straight at the two who were coming toward him. Astounded by his sudden appearance, they were bowled over before they knew what had happened. Yet as they fell, one went over backwards—directly in Tim's path.

Down Tim went on top of him. Next moment all three were struggling on the floor. Now a hullabaloo was rising behind them. Others were crowding through the doorway, rushing into the corridor. An overhead light flashed on. At last Tim broke free.

Desperately he leaped to his feet, fled toward the rear of the house, with the pack close on his heels. Up the stairs to the upper floor; down the length of one corridor and then into another, vainly seeking a place of refuge. Now shots were barking behind him—and sickeningly he realized that he was in a blind alley!

Ten feet more and he would come up against a blank wall....
The shots behind him had become a fusillade. Bullets whistled by his head, plucked at his flying coat, Tim whirled, to face the showdown—when suddenly a door at the end of the corridor opened. Maureen Durant, white-faced and wide-eyed, stood beckoning him inside....

CHAPTER 3
INVULNERABLE INVADERS

THE MORNING after the appalling attack on Philadelphia, America was a terrified nation. Fear was in every eye—fear that was the more terrible because no man knew just what it was he feared. Destruction and death, yes—but from where? From somewhere up in the skies—from a place that was no more than a tiny dot of light in the darkest night.

Mars.... Men once had talked of Mars in the abstract, had been taught to list it as one of the planets—but it had never been *real* to them. Always it had been a semi-mythical place like the lost continent of Atlantis; like the Pliocene Age or the Stone

Age—something that might have been but that meant nothing to the average man.

And now suddenly it was actual. Now its strange inhabitants, whose very existence scientists had debated and denied, were hovering over the earth, ready to swoop clown and spread death and destruction without the slightest warning! Strange creatures who could walk through flames—who could murder but could not be killed!

Fearfully men's eyes turned upward, scanning the sky for a sign of the dread invaders. Helplessly they turned to one another for aid, for some means of combatting or escaping the doom that hung over them—and wherever they turned terror stared back at them.

"The Martians" was on everyone's lips—and each repetition of the name added impetus to the wildfire spread of the panic.

Philadelphia was not the only city that had been attacked. Half an hour after the descent on Broad Street, a leviathan of the air had swooped down on New York's Times Square and reduced it to a fire-gutted, corpse-strewn ruin. Fast on the heels of the radio bulletins from Philadelphia had come the news of the disaster in New York—and the demoralization of the panic-stricken nation was complete....

Haggard and tired-eyed after a night of sleepless activity, Jimmy Christopher faced the baffling problem next morning. Gathered in his office were those upon whom he had depended most heavily in times of stress: Diane Elliot, his fiancée; Nan Christopher, his twin sister; John Christopher, his gray-haired father, who once had been listed only as Q-6 on the roll of

American Intelligence; Norman King, the young scientist who headed the research laboratory that was now an invaluable adjunct of the War Department; and several of the assistants who had proved their worth in many a tight and desperate situation.

With them was a gray-haired, keen-eyed, distinguished figure who, a few years before, had been a New England manufacturer and now was President of the United States. Andrew Warren's frank face had been far more placid when he controlled only the destinies of his mills. Now there were lines of care in his forehead and cheeks. Wrinkles puckered the corners of his eyes, and constant anxiety lurked in their depths.

Andrew Warren's presidency had been a stormy one. Engrossed with the task of rebuilding and repairing the ravages of war, and constantly on the alert to drive off the treacherous onslaughts of covetous powers anxious to take advantage of that preoccupation—it often seemed that he had not slept at all during his more than three years in office. More than once he had felt that the burden was too heavy for him to carry, had felt that he must go down under it. Then the thought of Operator 5 giving his young life unreservedly to his country, struggling on indefatigably when it seemed that all hope was past, had shamed him and given him the strength to carry on.

More and more Andrew Warren had leaned on the head of his secret service when peril confronted the nation. More than once he had seen Operator 5 snatch victory and salvation out of what had seemed certain defeat. Each time Andrew Warren had told himself that this would be the last savage threat the nation would have to face, that now there would be peace—and each time disaster had suddenly confronted them from nowhere.

But it had never been quite so baffling, so horrible, as this. Philadelphia and New York raided in one night—without so much as a shred of evidence to indicate from whence the savage invaders had come....

A sigh that Warren could not repress escaped from his lips as he turned to where Operator 5 was questioning a tall, thin-faced young man who had arrived that morning from New York. "**IT WAS** about five minutes to nine," Herbert Carrol was saying; "I am certain about that because Bea had made her first entrance. The chorus was backstage, and Bea was just finishing her first number when fifteen or sixteen of those strange-look-ing creatures came out from the wings on both sides. They all looked alike—red, rubbery-looking sort of uniforms and great, round heads that were three or four times too large for their bodies. They swarmed out on the stage and grabbed the girls.

"Of course, I had seen the dress rehearsal of the show, and there had been no such number in it—but the whole thing was so bizarre that I thought it must be a last-minute innovation that had been added. That was what everyone else thought. They laughed and applauded when the girls screamed. But when one of those creatures grabbed Bea and her terrified shriek rang through the house I suddenly knew that I was watching no make-believe.

"The audience began to understand at the same moment. They started up from their seats uncertainly, but before they could make a move those red creatures had lifted the girls in their arms and carried them through the wings. I rushed to the front of the theater to get to the stage door—and when I stepped out into the street I thought I must be mad.

"People were streaming through Forty-fifth Street in such a panic as I had never seen—and behind them was what seemed to be a solid wall of flame. All of Times Square was blazing like a huge bonfire. I ran back to the stage door and up to the dressing-rooms—but Bea and the rest of the girls were gone. The rooms were empty except for the dead bodies of three of the male members of the cast.

"By that time the whole theater was in an uproar. People were rushing out and then trying to fight their way back inside when they saw what was happening on the street. I managed to get out and entered the Hotel Astor through the back door. Everything was wild panic in there, but I got up to one of the upper floors and looked out over Broadway. Only for a few moments—but that was sufficient. It looked just as if someone had painted every side of the square with liquid fire. Flames licked up the face of every building. Even the fire hydrants and the iron fence in the center of the square were burning—not to mention the dead bodies that lay wherever I looked."

"And you saw nothing more of Miss Halliday?" Jimmy Christopher prompted when Carrol's voice lowered and then stopped entirely.

"Yes—I caught just one glimpse of her," the New Yorker said huskily. "Just as she was dragged into the huge airship that stood in the middle of the square. The light fell full on her face for a moment. She was screaming wildly. That was the last I saw of her—the last I ever will see of her…."

His eyes were stricken, his lips trembling. But suddenly his jaw clenched and he sat bolt upright.

"I want to fight those devils, Operator 5!" he cried. "That is why I came to Washington. To tell you what I saw and to volunteer for any duty that will give me a chance to avenge what they have done to Bea Halliday. This was her first good role," his voice became bitter. "She worked so hard to make sure that it would be a success—and now it's all over…."

There were other eyewitnesses, dozens of them; but they had nothing new to add to Herbert Carrol's poignant recital. When it was finished Jimmy tried to avoid the young fellow's anguished, grimly probing eyes. He knew what Carrol had suffered; knew the avid thirst for revenge that tortured him. But what could he or anyone else say that would assuage that pain?

Two of America's largest cities had been hellishly attacked on the same night. In both cases the invaders' ship had vanished into the darkness. That was all he knew—all, except the practical certainty that they would return. Their second coming would be even more frightful….

These attacks, Operator 5 felt certain, were designed simply to spread a wild panic that would disorganize any attempt at resistance; and already they were having the desired effect. Already the migration from the big cities had begun. Those who were able to leave were fleeing to the country—anywhere where the dread invaders would not be able to find them.

Under government orders, the radio announcers were now

doing their best to reassure those who remained—were making every effort to discredit and minimize the Martian scare. But to try to reason with a terrified populace was a difficult task, especially when there was no concrete explanation to give them.

"Those invaders could not have been Martians," President Warren worded the thought that was in Operator 5's mind. "Profession McClurg, of the Rockefeller Foundation; Doctor Opdyke, of the Smithsonian Institute; Burhenne, of the University of Chicago—I spoke to them all this morning. They are unanimous in declaring that the planet Mars is uninhabited."

"And if it were inhabited, the Martians would not be using our firearms," Jimmy added. "I saw a pistol in the hand of one of those creatures. *He* was no Martian. But if not Martians, who are they?" he asked. "I have tried to think of every possibility—even that pacifist rally in Philadelphia. We heard that they had something up their sleeves. But it is hardly possible that they would slay thousands of their own followers—for what purpose?"

That question was answered surprisingly. As if the words were a cue, the door opened and Tim Donovan stepped into the conference room with Maureen Durant. For a moment his freckled face was wreathed in a grin as he shook hands with Jimmy and was surrounded by his friends. Then the smile vanished and Tim introduced the girl. Between them, they outlined what had occurred in the convention hall and in Overbrook Hills.

"I know that my father and brother had nothing to do with such a plot," Maureen finished. "We do not believe in war, but we are no traitors. Myron Sumner has been tricking us. He has been using the sincere pacifist leaders to mask this rebellion he was organizing. How far his plans have extended, I have no idea."

Andrew Warren watched her earnest face, and her words seemed to pile up on his shoulders, weigh them down.

"So this is it," he said softly. "This is the *coup* we were to expect. Now we are faced not only by an incomprehensible invasion from God only knows where but also with a rebellion within our very borders! I am almost tempted to let Sumner have his way, to let him match his wits against this menace—"

That bitter reflection was cut short by the sudden blast of a siren that wailed an eerie warning. For a moment they sat there transfixed, staring at one another—and in every face the same thought was mirrored. It had come! The invaders had returned, and this time the national capital was to experience the fiery scourge!

All over the city the warning sirens were wailing like lost souls—Washington bidding its inhabitants to find refuge from the horror against which it could not protect them. The mournful wail stole into the room; seemed to grip and hold them there. JIMMY CHRISTOPHER was the first to shake off its effect. Springing to his feet, he ran to the phone and impatiently jiggled the hook. There was no answer. Either the telephone exchange was already destroyed or the operators had fled for their lives.

With Tim Donovan and two of his men at his back, Jimmy hurried to the street. Here he was confronted by a scene of utter panic. Men and women were running, frantically. Cars, busses, even trucks, were dashing past at top speed, all caution and regard for regulations thrown to the wind.

It would have been useless to try to question any of those terror-goaded fugitives, but that was not necessary. Jimmy led the way in the direction from which they were coming—toward the beautiful Capitol Building that had risen on the ruins of the historic structure destroyed by the hordes of the Purple Empire.

Even before they reached a point from which they could view the wide plaza in front of the Capitol they could hear the roar of the flames and see the clouds of dense smoke that billowed upward. The Capitol was on fire—and so were the buildings on all sides of Constitution Plaza! Flames were holding carnival in that great square, feeding upon the stone buildings, the trees, upon the very sidewalks!

And there, in the midst of the raging conflagration, was the great rocket-ship Jimmy had seen in Philadelphia. Surrounded by hundreds of red-garbed, huge-headed creatures, the monster glided across the square on dozens of caterpillar treads that projected from its underside. As it went, blasts of grayish, almost invisible gas spurted from what appeared to be torpedo tubes in its prow and along its sides—gas that was shot into the air with sufficient force to carry it hundreds of yards before it spread out over everything that it touched.

Behind that gas barrage stalked the globe-headed men with their portable projectors—and wherever they turned their destructive rays fire broke out like magic. "So that is the secret of this incredible fire," Jimmy muttered, as he watched the destruction spread from building to building. "Those red outfits are fireproof, and those globes are filled with air that must be generated in them—and that is the answer to our supposed Martians."

But even though he understood how the destroyers operated, combatting them was another matter. To face the gas which belched from that air-monster was certain death—as the corpses which littered the plaza bore grisly witness. Those red-garbed devils were invulnerable—and yet, somehow they *must* be checked.

Somehow, they must be conquered, or they would lay waste to America from end to end.

Crouched there at one side of the plaza, Operator 5 grimly watched the destruction of the beautifully laid out park square that he had planned and helped to build. The Army Building, the Navy, the Treasury, the Department of State—one after the other these edifices went up in flames that feasted on marble and granite as if they had been no more than straw. Inexorable destruction that sent a chill down his spine as he read in it a symbolical foreshadowing of the devastation that would overwhelm the nation that he had helped to reconstruct from a ruined waste....

But that *must* not be!

These were no super-men. They were human beings armed with devilishly powerful weapons—but they were *not* invincible. They could be stopped. They could be killed the same as any other vandals. The terror they inspired ran ahead of them and wiped out all opposition before they had to face it.

That abject flight must be halted!

From the side doors of the burning departmental buildings,

he saw men darting, saw them turn to look back bitterly at
the destruction and then flee helplessly. Those men were not
cowards. Their faces were hard and set: the faces of men who

By sheer weight of numbers they bore the creature down!

longed to fling themselves upon these invaders. But they had no weapons, no possible chance against that flame-spewing host.

"God, if only we could do *something* to stop it!" Tim Donovan's fervent words were a prayer in his ear—a prayer that spurred Jimmy Christopher to desperate action.

"We *will* stop it!" he gritted, as he backed from his sheltered position and led the way on a run back to the next avenue. "We *must* stop it!" he repeated doggedly. They came to a halt. "Otherwise America is doomed! But we need weapons and we need men. I am going after the weapons. I leave it to you to recruit the men.

"You, Baker—" he turned to one of his assistants—"you know most of the men in the War Department Building. There are plenty of them still inside. Get in there and line them up. Ellis, you tackle the Navy Building. Tim will stay here to take charge of the men you send out to him."

Then he was gone; was racing down the street to one parked automobile after the other, until he found one with the ignition key still in place. Quickly he sprang behind the wheel and headed downtown.

ALREADY WASHINGTON looked like a ghost city. All activity had stopped: had been dropped at a moment's notice. Stores were empty, partly unloaded trucks stood abandoned at curbs, street-cars were left deserted in the middle of the block. Usually thronged thoroughfares were as empty as if the hour were midnight instead of almost noon.

Straight to the telephone exchange Jimmy drove. The building was deserted but still had the indefinable feeling of human occupancy; as if the operators had merely stepped away from their switchboards, momentarily. The little lights that signalized unanswered calls still glowed on the boards, and low buzzers clamored for attention.

Jimmy slipped into one of the seats and clamped the ear-phone over his head, the transmitter on his chest. Swiftly his eyes scanned the big board and he plugged in his number—listened tensely. Thank God the line was still in operation!

"Fort Sheridan," the military operator's voice announced from the army post just outside the capital.

"Colonel Matthews—as fast as you can get him!" Jimmy snapped. "This is Operator 5—on urgent business!"

It seemed ages before the gruff voice of the old soldier came over the wire. He was surprised, curious at the urgent summons, and Jimmy realized at once that he had no knowledge of the disaster that had befallen Washington. Quickly he outlined what had happened.

"We can fight them, Matthews—we *have* to fight them!" he followed up before the colonel could ask questions. "I need weapons and ammunition. A truck-load of hand-grenades and the largest mobile guns you can rush to us. But hurry, man—hurry, or there will be no city left to fight for!"

The connection snapped off, and then another was plugged in—the Pershing air-base, where Washington's aerial protectors were housed. Again Operator 5 rapid-fired his story the moment the commander picked up the phone.

"We need every plane you can get into the air, Blendow," he finished, while the astounded officer was still sputtering in amazement. "The bombers are most important. I doubt that machine-guns will have any effect on that ship. Our only hope is to tear it apart with high-explosives. That is all—but, for God's sake, hurry!"

Hurry…. It was easy to say, but the army post and the air-base were miles from the center of Washington. It would take time for them to respond. Would the invaders remain that long—or would they disappear again into the blue, satisfied with the destruction already inflicted?

That destruction was spreading. Even before Jimmy got back to the point where he had left his men, he met Tim Donovan, now with a force of nearly two hundred recruits who were backing away from the on-rushing flames. Two hundred desperate, grim-faced men who had armed themselves with pistols, clubs, even missiles—anything that could be used as a weapon.

A great cheer went up when they recognized Operator 5—and an even louder cheer, a few minutes later, when the first of the army bombers soared overhead and began to drop their deadly eggs into Constitution Plaza. At last America was fighting back! That spirit was contagious, and Jimmy had all he could do to restrain his men; to hold them in check until a light army truck loaded with hand grenades, came careening to a stop beside them.

That truck was the advance guard of the big eight-inch guns that came rumbling after it. Colonel Matthews was in personal command. On Jimmy Christopher's advice he ordered the big guns to converge on the plaza from three sides, while the grenade-armed volunteers would attempt a sortie to attract the attention of the invaders.

"We can't get sufficiently close to reach them with grenades," Jimmy decided swiftly. "Our best chance is to man these buildings in their path. The Commerce Building will be the next to go—that's our best bet!"

Eagerly they swarmed into the big structure that housed the Department of Commerce offices. There Jimmy divided them and assigned them to the various floors, gave them last-minute orders.

"Stay concealed behind the windows until they are within reach," he warned. "Then let them have it!"

There was not long to wait. Already the rocket-ship was belching gas at the front of the building, and now the red-garbed raiders were closing in, their projectors aiming. Instantly the front of the building was sheathed in flames. But now the windows were smashed out, and through them came a hail of grenades.

That stopped the globe-headed creatures in their tracks. Two of them went down and lay still. Their companions stooped and picked them up quickly. But now the defenders knew that these invaders could be overcome. The air-monsters were retreating, starting back toward their ship—and that precipitated the disaster!

Swept away by their enthusiasm, the defenders were leaping up from concealment, were leaving their positions and racing downstairs into the street, pursuing the invaders in their eagerness to get within throwing reach. Casting aside their momentary advantage, they were rushing straight to their deaths!

Jimmy watched that suicidal charge with stricken eyes. Already the wily invaders were turning, leveling their deadly projectors. Frantically he leaped out onto the ledge outside the second-story window where he was stationed and shouted to them.

"No! No! Fall back!" his voice rang out above their cheers. But they did not seem to hear him.

The projectors went into action—and flame leaped over those reckless chargers, like a flash of lightning. In an instant those doomed men were human, racing bonfires. Not only the volunteers, either. With agonized eyes Jimmy saw that disaster had also enveloped Colonel Matthews' men. The big guns were on fire—blazing as if they were tallow candles!

Out there in the middle of the plaza the invulnerable rocket-ship was still unscathed. Operator 5's plan had failed—had only brought death to those men who had trusted and followed him!

OVERWHELMED BY defeat, Jimmy stood out there on the ledge. He did not see the projectors that were now trained upon him. But Raymond Ellis saw them. Ellis had been one of the leaders of that fatal charge, but had whirled in time to avoid the fire-kindling ray that probed after him. He had started back toward safety when he saw those projectors shift their aim, saw them trained up on the ledge—on the leader who more than once had heroically saved his life....

Ellis stopped short, and in that split-second was doomed. One of the rays caught him and he burst into flames—but not before his grenade sailed back straight at the burning building and exploded directly beneath the second-story ledge.

The heavy stone ledge seemed to swell, seemed to raise several feet in the air as it disintegrated—and Jimmy went with it. For a moment he seemed to hang suspended in mid-air; then he was thrown back through the window and his men dragged him to safety. It was only momentary safety—for now the invaders had turned and were coming forward again, stalking toward the building.

"Downstairs!" Jimmy shouted quickly as he withdrew his men from the windows. "We'll be trapped in these upper floors."

Once on the ground floor, he hesitated, seemed on the verge of disobeying his own order to retreat as he looked back into the flaming plaza.

"If only we could get hold of one of those devils," he yearned aloud as he eyed the oncoming invaders. "If only we had one of them to show to the nation—"

"We can catch one," a low voice spoke in his ear, and he turned to find Diane Elliot there beside him. "I can trap one of them for you, Jimmy. They are all woman-hungry—we know that from Philadelphia and New York. The minute I show myself they will make a grab for me and then I can lead them straight to you."

As she spoke, she snatched off her hat and shook out her curly chestnut hair. Before Jimmy could stop her she had run to the blazing doorway and was darting out into the street!

"Diane!" his horrified cry pursued her. But she did not turn.

Out into that seething conflagration, she ran; to pause there, startled, when she saw the red-garbed destroyers advancing upon her. For a moment she seemed to be paralyzed with horror. Then a little scream burst from her lips and she turned back to the entrance—but not before one of the invaders was almost on top of her.

After her he pounded, one arm outstretched eagerly to grab her—and then Jimmy and his men were upon him. By sheer weight of numbers they bore the creature down and held him on the floor, while they lashed his arms and legs with belt-straps they held ready. The projector was knocked from his hand. A pistol was wrenched from his fingers before he had a chance to use it—and then he was helpless, threshing futilely.

Out in the plaza the huge rocket-ship was filling the air with its piercing whistle. Into its doorways flocked the recalled invaders. And with a deafening roar the mammoth craft zoomed off into space to escape the hail of bombs that was now raining down upon it from the army planes circling at a safe distance overhead....

CHAPTER 4
THE MAN FROM WHERE?

MOST OF the government buildings and a good part of the city of Washington had been destroyed before the invaders were driven off and the firemen could get the blaze under control. But the research laboratory which Dr. Norman King had established in the basement of the War Department Building had been constructed to meet just such emergencies. It was fireproof and bombproof. Even though the floors above it were reduced to charred wreckage, his laboratory had come through the test intact.

It was there that Operator 5 took his prisoner, and there that he summoned a group of experts to inspect the curious invader.

The man seemed nearest to an Oriental, or a Eurasian. They saw that the moment they removed the remarkably light but unbreakable metal helmet that covered his over-large head. His skin was a pale yellow, his features broad and yet not flat, his dark eyes narrow and slightly almond-shaped—a perplexing mingling of characteristics that might have been Mongolian and Caucasian.

But it was his large, globular head that was most surprising. It made him look like a freak, a monstrosity—and yet that apparently was a racial characteristic of all the invaders.

The foremost ethnologists of the Smithsonian Institute gathered in that laboratory to study and question him, but his nationality or racial group baffled them. They tried him with Japanese and with a dozen Chinese dialects, but he seemed to understand nothing they said. His face was a blank, his eyes expressionless—until one of the experts asked his question in the language of the Tibetan lamas.

For an instant the dark eyes flickered, narrowed ever so slightly in an effort to make them appear non-committal—but the alert questioner had caught that telltale muscular contraction.

"You *are* a Tibetan!" he snapped. "You may pretend not to understand, but you know what I am saying. You have given yourself away."

But again the dark eyes were as blank and expressionless as those of a corpse. Whether or not the prisoner understood, he would not admit his nationality—would give them no slightest hint of why or from where he and his fellows had swooped down upon America. For an hour the experts persisted, but at last they had to give up and admit their bafflement.

"He is a Tibetan—or a member of one of the tribes that inhabit the desolate western regions of China," pronounced the ethnologist who had evoked that only betrayal of interest. "But how those wild, half-savage creatures came into possession of a rocket-ship is something more than I can even attempt to imagine!"

When the scientists had gone, Operator 5 felt that their help had made the problem even more mystifying, if that were possible. A Tibetan, from the desert wilderness of Central Asia, now here on the Atlantic seaboard of North America—that was too fantastic! And yet, in this emergency, he could afford to overlook no possible clue. If the solution to this mystery lay in Asia, in Asia it must be found.

Asia....

Swiftly he reviewed the members of his far-flung organization—trusted, capable men who served America loyally at home and abroad. Lee Morton and George Keyes were in Shanghai. John Willard was in Hong Kong, Ed Burchell in Manila. Arthur Tolman was on a tanker that would dock in Yokohama this week. Jim Addison and Tom Noyes—that made seven; two for Japan and five to cover China and penetrate into Tibet....

The code cablegrams he would send them were already taking shape in his mind, but before he left the laboratory he stopped to watch Norman King and his assistants experimenting upon the red uniform and the metal helmet they had taken from the captive. That peculiar covering, which had fitted the invader like thick, loose skin, proved to be made of a strange silk and rubber compound. Fastened by zippers that worked from the inside and were covered with overlapping flaps, the effect was of one unbroken stretch of material from chin to feet.

"Bullet-proof silk is its basis," King announced. "But there is something more to it than that. Something that makes it fire-proof as well. From what you tell me of the gas the rocket ship expelled, and from the way it set fire to steel and stone, it probably is something that becomes highly combustible when fused with carbon. This material must be treated with something that will resist it—"

"And that's what we need if we are to have any chance against these invaders!" Jimmy was quick to see where he was leading.

"Locate that for me, Doc—and we'll have these murdering raiders by the throat!"

"This laboratory will not be darkened until we do," King said quietly; and when Jimmy Christopher went out into the smoking, smouldering desolation that had been the center of the United States capitol, he felt that there was some hope.

THE RADIO had broadcast reassuring bulletins, and Washington was coming out of its cellars by the time he left the laboratory and started toward his office. In the tense excitement of the morning and the aftermath with Norman King, he had had little time to consider the news Tim Donovan had brought from Philadelphia. Now the significance of what probably was going on at Overbrook Hills came home to him with full force, to add fresh worries to his burden.

He glanced at his watch. It was three o'clock. Plenty of time for Myron Sumner to have gone into action; and Washington had been cut off from the rest of the world for hours. Much could have happened during that time....

How much had happened, he learned the moment he stepped into his office, just as John Christopher was putting the telephone back into its cradle. The grave faces of Diane Elliot and Tim Donovan, the shamed countenance of Maureen Durant, were eloquent of trouble.

"Sumner has opened up, Jimmy," John Christopher said gravely. "His crowd struck at noon—in Philadelphia, Pittsburgh, Savannah, Atlanta and New Orleans. They are fighting in New York and Boston. Those are the only cities we have heard from so far, but there probably are more. They seem to have had this thing perfectly planned!"

"This invasion is perfect for them," Tim Donovan gritted. "It gave Sumner an excuse to stage his *coup,* and now it will give his renegades an opportunity to stab their country in the back. While decent men are trying to fight off the invaders, these rats will be seizing control of city after city until the whole nation is in their hands."

"No, Tim—they will not!" Jimmy Christopher's face was flushed with anger as he strode across the office and reached for the phone. "We're going to stop this rebellion and stop it quick! The White House, operator," he barked into the transmitter. "Operator 5 to speak with the President."

Andrew Warren must have been waiting for that call. His anxious voice came over the wire almost immediately. He knew of the nation-wide developments and had been in conversation with the governors of the disaffected states, had already endorsed the calling of the state militias.

"It is Philadelphia that concerns me, sir," Jimmy told him. "Overbrook Hills, in particular. Sumner may no longer be maintaining his headquarters in the Durant estate—but, unless I am greatly mistaken, he will be there. He will stay there to demonstrate his power. I am flying there immediately, and meanwhile I would like your authority to order the regular army to surround the place."

"You have it, Jimmy," Warren assented promptly. "You have full authority to take whatever measures you deem necessary. Only, take care of yourself. America needs you now more than ever. With these invaders harrying us from the skies, we can't afford to lose you because of Myron Sumner."

Jimmy Christopher had no intention of losing his life, but he did intend to settle with Myron Sumner at any cost. Ordinarily, this rebellion would have been of little importance. Most likely it would have petered out of its own accord. If not, it could have been systematically suppressed. But now, when the nation's every resource must be marshaled to fight off the invaders from the sky, Sumner's malcontents were striking at the very life of America. Now—they must all be smashed!

And there was one sure way to smash it....

Jimmy insisted that only Maureen Durant accompany him on that plane flight to Overbrook Hills. The task that lay before him was one he must handle alone, with Maureen simply there to launch him on his way.

BROAD STREET was a blackened scar in the center of Philadelphia, as they passed over it, but there were no visible marks of the rebellion that had carried the city almost without a struggle. Through his field-glasses Jimmy saw that arm-banded men with rifles over their shoulders patrolled the streets instead of the police. But there was no other sign of unusual activity— until Overbrook Hills lay beneath them and Maureen pointed out the estate that surrounded her home.

Jimmy focused his glasses on the thickly treed grounds— and suddenly grabbed for the air controls as a salvo of anti-aircraft shells burst around them. For a moment it was uncertain whether or not they would be able to climb and zigzag their way out of that swiftly closing trap. But Jimmy was no tyro at this game. He climbed swiftly, steadily gaining altitude on a crazy course that gave the gunners no chance to box the plane or to score a direct hit.

That anti-aircraft greeting had been swift, but the brief glimpse he had caught of the estate had revealed a military layout that would withstand days of siege. Sumner had studded the grounds with field-pieces and machine-gun nests; had made a veritable fortress of the place. In a short while the government troops that were already on the way would arrive and take up positions around it. They would be able to batter it into submission and carry it eventually—but, before it fell, hundreds, perhaps thousands, of lives would be lost.

While that siege was going on, Sumner's men would be pushing their conquest in a hundred cities—and all the time those unknown invaders hovered overhead like vultures, sweeping down at will to desolate the unprotected internecine American battle-ground....

Jimmy groaned aloud at the thought.

"I must get in there," he ground out grimly. "Right away—before the troops arrive. That's where you can help, Maureen." A plan formed swiftly in his churning brain. "Sumner does not know whether you left the estate willingly or not. The last glimpse he had of you I was dragging you into a car and racing off with you. Common sense should tell him that you aided me—but a man is likely to believe what he wants to. And I don't think that Myron Sumner wants to believe that you would turn against him. We're going to get a car, and you are going to drive back home and tell him that you managed to escape from me."

61

Maureen's hazel eyes snapped with excitement.

"If we can get past the guards at the entrance—if I can get into the grounds—I can get you into the house," she nodded quick agreement.

In a field some ten miles beyond Overbrook Hills, Jimmy managed a landing. Close by was a large garage he had spotted from above. Here he was able to hire a coupé that the proprietor used in answering trouble calls on the road. The trunk space in the rear was jammed with tools and repair materials of every sort—which made it ideal for Operator 5's purpose.

A few miles from the garage, Jimmy pried open the lock and set to work unloading. When he was finished, he was wedged on the floor beneath the seats, covered with layers of garage paraphernalia of every sort, and Maureen had taken his place at the wheel. Once more the car started up, settling the greasy rubbish down tight upon him as it sped toward Overbrook Hills and the test that might mean his death.

"Good luck, Operator 5!" Jimmy heard the girl bid him softly, and then the car turned in at the driveway.

They had arrived! Now he could hear men's voices; could hear one of them greet Maureen; could hear her gasping a hurried story of her escape. He heard the back of the car being opened, then the cover dropping back into place as the investigator turned away.

"Don't bother to come in with me. I'll drive right into the garage," he heard Maureen say, and again the car rolled forward over a crushed stone road, over a smooth stretch, and then came to a stop.

Quickly Maureen stepped out and came to the back. The cover opened and she started pulling out the piled-up repair litter. Jimmy helped her as soon as he could free his hands, and then he was out beside her on the floor of the big, two-story garage.

"This way." Swiftly she led the way to a back room and pointed to a doorway. "There it is—our rainy-weather entrance," she whispered. "It leads you to the basement. I'll go in the front way, and if there is any way that I can help—"

The sound of footsteps at the front of the garage silenced her. Quickly she hurried back to the car, and Jimmy stepped through the doorway onto a flight of steps that led down to a concrete-walled tunnel. The basement of the big house was empty when he reached it, but there was the sound of many footsteps on the floor above.

CAUTIOUSLY HE ascended the steps and turned the knob of the door at their head. Warily he opened it and stepped into the corridor at the rear of the house. It was quiet there. These were the domestic quarters, now deserted. The kitchen, pantry, then a wardrobe room with outfits for the cook, maids—for the butler!

Here was the answer! Shirt, collar, tie, vest and coat—they would fit him well enough! This disguise would enable him to escape detection for a few moments, until he could locate Sumner....

That was not difficult. The pseudo-pacifist had established his office in what apparently had been Seymour Durant's library. Twice Jimmy passed it, as he marched down the corridor on imaginary errands. Both times there were men in consultation with Sumner—and then finally the traitor was alone!

Without a word Jimmy stepped through the doorway and turned unhurriedly to close the door behind him. As if it were part of his daily ritual, he turned the key in the lock—and then whirled to face Sumner with an automatic that had leaped magically from his shoulder holster.

But Myron Sumner was no dullard. He sensed his danger and reacted to it with lightning speed. There was no time to reach for a gun, but his fingers closed on the heavy paper-weight at his elbow, hurled it across the room as he threw himself back from the desk.

That hurtling missile caught Jimmy on the wrist and sent a spasm of pain shooting up his arm. The gun dropped from his half-paralyzed fingers—and then Sumner came at him in a flying tackle.

Jimmy lashed out with an uppercut that connected with Sumner's jaw—but the blow had no power behind it. Jimmy's injured wrist crumpled at the contact; seemed to be mashed into a pulp of torn flesh and splintered bones. Sumner shook his head, and a flash of triumph glinted in his eyes. His fists smashed at Jimmy's head, pounded into his stomach—and then his big arms opened wide for a bear-hug grip. Just in time Jimmy avoided that trap.

Darting back for an instant, he leaped in again—and this time his good arm closed around Sumner's neck, twisted his head backward as his right leg slipped between Sumner's and caught one of them in a tight lock. Every muscle straining to

64

the utmost, perspiration pouring out on their faces, they grappled desperately... but gradually Jimmy gained the upper hand.

Now his still painful right arm was slipping behind Sumner's shoulder, under his armpit; was tightening in a wrestling grip that had once put even the great Zbysko in serious trouble. That grip tightened remorselessly, and Sumner's eyes popped wide, filled with sudden fear. The grip would break his neck, and he knew it.

When he met the cold stare of Jimmy Christopher's steely eyes, Sumner knew that there was to be no reprieve, no mercy. This was to be his death—his execution!

"No—no, Operator 5!" he gasped. "I give up—I yield. I surrender for every man at my command—I swear it. If you kill me, someone else will only take my place. If you take me at my word—I can handle my crowd. I will swing them to you, make them fight for you instead of against you—"

Operator 5's relentless grip halted. For a long moment he looked deep into the fellow's eyes and weighed that proposition. And because he was no killer—because he preferred to win his fellow-men to his support instead of annihilating them—he took Myron Sumner's word.

The deadly grip relaxed, and Sumner staggered free, to mop his sweat-beaded brow with a handkerchief while he gasped for breath.

"I meant it, Operator 5," he repeated earnestly, when he had recovered. "I really am glad that you bested me. You forced me to do what I wanted to—and wasn't man enough to do myself. I know that this is no time for internal strife. I know what America faces—and I have the men and equipment you need so badly. I have a well armed organization in almost every large city, and I can make them the nucleus of your defense, a bulwark for the defense of America—if you will let me.

"Let me join your staff," he proposed. "I swear loyalty and promise to follow you faithfully. And that goes for my entire organization. If they know that I am in your confidence, that I am associated with you, there will be no difficulty handling them."

Operator 5's hand went out, and they sealed that compact.

In that room where death had almost settled their feud, they sat down to plan a nation-wide defense against the invaders— and when Jimmy Christopher's plane headed back to Washington a new hopefulness rode with him. With Norman King working to solve the riddle of the invaders' flame gas and their protection against it, and with Myron Sumner bending his efforts to convert his organization of former trouble-makers into watchful Minute Men, the threat that had seemed so appalling was beginning to fade, beginning to lose some of its terror....

THAT NIGHT the dread rocket-ship swooped down into the center of Boston Common. When it disappeared again into the upper darkness, more than a quarter of the city was in flames and the list of the dead ran into the thousands.

All of New England shuddered in terror—and then was convulsed with wild panic when the long distance wires brought a frenzied plea for help from stricken Providence. The invaders had landed in Exchange Place and were setting the whole city on fire! That desperate plea was abruptly cut short in the middle—and it was not until morning that the nation learned that more than half of Rhode Island's capitol city had been wiped off the map!

With the appalling stories of death and destruction from these raided cities came reports of wholesale migration from all of New England. From Maine to Florida, the Atlantic seaboard shivered in dread apprehension of a visit from the "Martians". In desperation Jimmy went to the radio and tried to stem the tide of panic.

"These invaders are no visitors from another world," he sent his plea out onto the air. "They are human beings like the rest of us. We have captured one of them and are now working night and day to combat the weapons they are using against us. Their attacks are intended to throw you into a panic and make you rush from your homes. I plead with you not to be stampeded. If you run away now, this terror will spread wider and pursue you.

"Of the women I ask this—stay in your homes and keep your families off the streets, ready to take refuge below ground when the alarm sirens sound. Of the men I ask this—report to your local defense committees and take your part in fighting these barbarous invaders who are attempting to desolate our land. Fighting shoulder to shoulder we can defeat them and drive them back whence they came!"

Yet for once his persuasive voice seemed to have lost its magic. Not even their faith in Operator 5 could still their panic and combat the fearful stories of supernatural menace that were speeding from lip to lip.

Within three days the big cities of the East lost nearly half of their populations, and the highways were thronged with hungry, homeless thousands fleeing to they knew not where. Even the national government crossed the Potomac and took up its headquarters in Alexandria, where President Warren commandeered a score of mansions for his burned-out department staffs.

During those three days Jimmy Christopher strove tirelessly to locate the lair of the invaders. Convinced that they must operate from a hiding-place somewhere in the East, he instituted a search of every state east of the Mississippi and even enlisted the aid of the Governor-General of Canada. Myron Sumner's militant units lived up to all he had promised in that search. They scoured the Eastern states from end to end—but the result was complete failure.

Hartford, New Haven and Portland felt the fury of the fiery scourge during those nights—and always the strange invaders swept down out of nowhere to commit their deviltry and then streaked back into the unknown. If only they could be located, if only they offered something visible and concrete to fight, Jimmy was certain that he could rally the nation. It was this haunting fear of the unknown, this enervating dread of the supernatural, that was shattering the morale of even the bravest....

By the end of that third day he knew that his every effort had failed. The location of the rocket-ship was as much a secret as on the night it made its first appearance in Philadelphia. Yet, surely, *someone* must see a monster that size in its comings and goings. *Someone* must know where it was located, where its crew secured their supplies.

Desperately he turned once more to the radio.

"These invaders who are despoiling our country and slaughtering our citizens are right here somewhere in our midst," he told all who were listening for the latest bulletins of the scourge. "They have a secure hiding-place, but sooner or later somebody is certain to discover it. If you have any clue to the whereabouts of this air-monster, if you have noticed anything peculiar in your neighborhood which might mean that the invaders are hiding out nearby, take your information to the nearest police official so that it can be forwarded to Operator 5!"

CHAPTER 5
DEATH'S LAIR

PERLEY HARBIN paced the floor of his big kitchen and cursed the fact that he did not have a telephone. Back and forth, back and forth—until the sounds coming from the bed-chamber, on the other side of the living-room, halted him and sent little chills creeping up and down his broad back. His big hands clenched and unclenched helplessly, and then once more he took refuge in the darkness outside.

Where was Dr. Stevens? Why didn't he come? It was more than two hours since Jim Bunce, the hired man, drove off in Perley's Ford to notify him. Two hours—and neither Stevens nor Bunce had returned from Bartlett, which was a half-hour trip, even for the asthmatic Ford.

Vainly Harbin's eyes quested the dark road. There was no glimmer of headlights; not a light of any sort in the darkness that had settled down over the New Hampshire hills. He shivered, but not from the nip of chill that tinged the early September night air; again he had caught that low moan from the bedroom.

Dora was in there, facing the ordeal she had prepared to meet so bravely. Her sister Thelma and Perley's mother were with her, but Dr. Stevens ought to be there. Somehow, Perley felt as though the physician's absence was some fault of his own—felt that he had betrayed Dora in the moment when she needed him most.

Back inside he went, half-tempted to go to her—but the living-room doorway was as far as he got. There his courage failed, and again he started to pace the kitchen—that spotless kitchen with its rows of shiny pots and pans, with the new stove and furnishings that had been in place little more than a year. The memory of Dora's happiness when she arranged them for the first time rose up to choke him, to bring a mistiness before his eyes—a mist that the cool air outside would dispel.

Still there was no sign of Stevens. Still the road was dark; all the valley except his little cottage was dark. But no—now there was a flicker of light off in the direction of Ben Mouseley's place. Perley's heart leaped. That was the direction from which Stevens would come. Keenly he studied the increasing radiance, but a puzzled frown settled over his well tanned, square-jawed face.

That flickering yellow light did not come from the headlights of a car—it was the mounting glow of flames. Mouseley's place was nearly a mile away, and yet that radiance was crimsoning the sky!

The countryman's urge to rush to the assistance of his neighbor at the dread sign of fire was strong upon Perley Harbin. But he could not leave now. He couldn't leave Dora at such a time. Tortured by his impotence, he stood staring at the reddening sky—until a sound close by now snapped his thoughts back to home.

It sounded like a footstep scraping on the path…. But it couldn't be. Perley peered into the darkness and listened intently. There was nothing. Puzzled, he walked back to the barn—but, as he expected, all was silent there. Must have been his imagination, he concluded, as he went slowly back to the house. Anxious to see Stevens coming up the path, he was *imagining* he heard him….

But suddenly he stopped short, rooted to the ground by a shrill shriek that fairly stabbed into his brain. Dora's shriek—but not the regular kind. Perley needed no experience to tell him that the pangs of childbirth would wring no such cry from the lips of a woman.

That was a shriek of terror—a shrill scream that was dripping with horror!

Wrenching himself out of the trance that held him transfixed, he pounded up to the house and flung himself through the kitchen door, across the living-room and into the bedroom—to stand there aghast at the sight that confronted him. Dora was lying back in the bed, her mouth slack, her eyes wide and staring, her whole face twisted into a mask of terror!

She was dead! He knew that even before he walked stiffly to the bedside, even before he lifted her limp hand. And the other two in the room—his mother and his sister-in-law—they looked as if they were dead, too; as if they were corpses stand-

71

ing there and staring at the very gates of hell now open before their horrified eyes.

"It was there—at the window!" Thelma gasped. "One of those Martians! It looked right in at us! Dora saw it! Oh, Dora!"

Her heart-broken sob was pierced by a scream from the older woman at her side; a scream of terror that whirled Perley around from the bed. Before his eyes flashed to his mother he saw what had torn that scream from her lips—saw it too late to save himself.

There, rushing through the doorway from the living-room, was a weird-looking, crimson-hued creature with a great metal globe for a head! And behind him came another!

They were upon Harbin before he could move, before he could set himself to meet their onslaught. Desperately he grappled with the leader. But a fist that felt like a hammer pounded down on his head. His senses spun dizzily; he could feel his knees buckling. Blindly, helplessly, he struck out with his fists—but another blow lifted him from his feet and slapped him back against the wall before he finally sagged to the floor.

Those blows would have disposed of the average man for several hours. But Perley Harbin was tough—the heritage of years of plowing and wood-chopping. On the very brink of unconsciousness, he clung doggedly to his senses. Dimly, through a dizzy, sickening fog, he saw his mother faint; saw one of those fantastic-looking creatures grab Thelma and drag her to the doorway....

Her pretty face was stained with blood where the creature

had struck her when she tried to fight him off. Her terror-risen voice sobbed a hopeless prayer for help.

That agonized plea tapped a well of fresh strength in Perley's half-numbed body; enabled him to crawl after them on hands and knees—to get to his feet when he reached the outer door. They were carrying Thelma away, taking her off into the darkness. He could just see her light-colored dress in the glow from the windows. Blindly he plunged after it, ran halfway across the yard and grabbed at the creature who clutched her.

His hand no more than touched the cold, slick-feeling shoulder than the creature whirled and lashed out at him savagely. The red fist caught him full in the face and fairly lifted him from his feet. Back he staggered like a spinning tenpin—to reel into the flimsy housing around an old well, crash through it.

Down into the shaft he plunged, and knew no more....

WHEN HARBIN came to his senses, his teeth were chattering and he was sitting in a pool of scummy water that reached halfway up his belly. The chill of it must have revived him—fairly quickly, he judged, as he fought the dizziness.

The well was pitch-dark, but the top was like a great yellow-red moon above him. That was queer. It could not yet be daylight, and daylight was never that livid color, was never shot through with live sparks. Sparks that meant fire.

The age-old challenge brought Perley to his feet. Reaching up with his fingers, he had no difficulty finding a purchase on the uneven stones. Slowly and tediously he climbed foot after foot, assailed by continual waves of nausea and already sick with horror at the foreknowledge of what he would find when he reached the top.

At last he pulled himself over the edge—and stared at what was left of his home. A blazing skeleton of rafters that toppled in upon itself and sent up a wild shower of sparks, almost the moment his head appeared. A seething furnace that was the death-pyre of his Dora and of his mother....

Dazedly, more like an automaton than a human being, he hoisted himself out of the well and got to his feet. Now he saw that his barn and chicken-house were gone, too. Only beds of glowing embers were left to show where they had stood. He was alone, stripped of all he loved, all he valued—and the fiends who had done this awful thing to him were gone....

Hardly knowing where he was going but motivated by some dazed idea of following them, he walked out to the dark road and started down the valley in the direction of Ben Mouseley's. The physical exertion of walking cleared the fog from his brain and began to bring him back to normal. Gradually he began to remember—and to understand.

That reddish glow in the sky in the direction of Mouseley's place—it had been a forerunner of the one that was to arise above his own little buildings. As he expected, when he reached the place where Ben Mouseley's house had stood he found nothing but a heap of ashes and smoldering embers. Not a sign of life, not a building that was still standing.

It was the same when he reached the Abner Tuttle place a quarter mile farther down the road. He found only ashes that had almost ceased to glow. Four more burned-out farmhouses he passed before he discovered why Dr. Stevens had failed to arrive after Jim Bunce had gone to fetch him. The smell of burned rubber and paint led him to a clump of bushes at the side of the road, where his Ford lay overturned, a fire-blackened ruin—with the hardly recognizable bodies of the doctor and the hired man pinned beneath it!

In a few short hours that valley had become a place of death, devastated from end to end! Every building had been burned, every man, woman and child carried off or murdered and tossed into the bonfire that consumed their homes!

Sick with horror, Perley stalked his way through the awful desolation that had enveloped a peaceful countryside. Nowhere did he find a sign of life—until he reached a point a few hundred yards from where the valley road merged with another that led out to the main highway. There, at last, he caught the gleam of headlights.

A car coming toward him. At last he would be able to talk to someone, to voice the unspeakable horrors he had endured. At last he would be able to get to Bartlett and tell his story to the authorities.

But suddenly two shots rang out just ahead of him—two orange flashes spurted from the side of the road. The car skidded wildly, swung halfway around with a squeal of brakes. Again the nocturnal stillness was torn by the bark of shots—and then the road was fairly alive with those red-garbed devils. The beam of the headlights made their huge heads seem even more monstrous, their smoothly-covered bodies more diabolical, as they swarmed over the machine and pushed it into a ditch.

The lights went out as it overturned—and then a new light routed the darkness as leaping flames licked over the car, hungrily.

Crouched low in the shadow of the trees, Perley Harbin watched those murdering fiends hover around their latest victim; watched them again melt into the darkness and resume their wolfish vigil. That road was closed, he realized. Evidently his valley and the wild section of hills, that extended beyond it, were now taboo to any but these weird creatures who had taken possession.

Perley longed to throw himself at those cold-blooded demons, to tear them limb from limb with his bare hands. But he realized that to attempt to attack them would be suicide, and he did not want to die yet. He wanted to live now more than ever before—wanted to live in order to exact a full measure of vengeance for Dora and the little one who had never seen the light of day....

Carefully he picked his way through the woods, detouring widely so that those lurking watchers would not detect him. At last he came out on a stretch of road far beyond them, and plodded along it to the highway. Soon the lights of Bartlett gleamed far off in the distance—a sleepy country village entirely oblivious to the horror that now stalked so close to its doors.

Instinctively Perley turned toward the welcoming lights of the hamlet's only tavern, seeking the company of his kind. But the taproom was empty, except for the bartender, who was twirling the dial of a radio—twirling it slowly... and then stopping to listen.

"If you have any clue to the whereabouts of this air-monster, if you have noticed anything peculiar in your neighborhood which might mean that the invaders are hiding out nearby, take your information to the nearest police official so that it can be forwarded to Operator 5," an urgent voice was just finishing the end of an impassioned plea.

"Where is the deputy sheriff—up at the house?" Perley asked, but the bartender shook his head discouragingly.

"Gone down to Concord," he added. "Won't be back till the end of the week—maybe not then."

There was no police official to go to; but Harbin's information *must* be forwarded to Operator 5!

Perley Harbin strode to the tavern's telephone booth and called the operator. The story that poured from his lips shocked her out of her usual lethargy. Excited voices came to him over the wire—voices that urged him to be patient, not to leave the phone. Voices that seemed to come from a great distance. Voice after voice... and finally then a calm, vibrant voice that announced:

"This is Operator 5. You have some information for me?... All right, now tell your story...."

JIMMY CHRISTOPHER had not left the broadcasting station when that call reached him. Curiously he lifted the receiver to his ear—and in a moment he was tingling with excitement. At last he had located the rocket-ship's nest. That could be the only answer to this death-quarantine that had been clamped down on Perley Harbin's valley! The rocket-ship was hidden somewhere in that northern New Hampshire wilderness!

Now all that remained was to discover the actual hide-out, and then to close in on the marauders and bomb them to extinction....

Jimmy commandeered an army plane for the trip to Bartlett that night and ordered a squadron to follow him in the morning. Then, later, with Perley Harbin in the cabin beside him, he led the search from the air. But the back-country, beyond Harbin's valley, proved to be a tangled wilderness of hills and gullies that led up to the White Mountains. To negotiate much of that country on foot would take searchers days, perhaps weeks. The parties that went into it made slow progress... and the results from the air finally proved to be no more satisfactory. Dangerously close to deceptive-looking gullies and treacherous stretches of forest, the planes swooped, yet nowhere was there a sign of the mammoth rocket-ship. Nowhere did they catch sight of the red-clad invaders. From one end to the other, Perley Harbin's valley was pocked with the black ruins of burned homes. But beyond that new-made desolation was a wilderness that seemed primeval.

Somewhere in those ragged hills and valleys, Jimmy felt certain, the rocket-ship had found a secure hideout—but *where?* That question still was unanswered at the end of the third day, when the defeated planes headed back to Washington. And meanwhile the destruction had been going on unabated, the raided area spreading out until it covered most of New England. New London, Bangor, Springfield, Manchester, Lowell, Lewiston—nightly the list of fire-scourged cities grew longer. Now the flames raged unchecked, the depleted fire departments no longer able to cope with them.

In less than a week thickly populated Massachusetts and Connecticut were almost drained of their citizens. A vast, fire-blackened desert spread out wider and wider over that great manufacturing area and began to move westward into New York.

Operator 5 watched, with mounting desperation, the spread of that nation-paralyzing desolation. To be right there within reach of the invaders and not to be able to find them drove him nearly frantic. They were somewhere in that wilderness— he *knew* that. Yet the most expert guides returned from their searching to report nothing but failure.

Yet they *were* in there—and at last Jimmy hit upon a way to reach them! A way to reach the hide-out with a better guide than any of those who were stilt scouring the whole region as far north as the Canadian border. He would make the invaders lead him to the ship themselves!

Jimmy Christopher's clean-cut handsome face was thoroughly, solidly masculine, but his features were so regular and well formed that he would have found it easy, with stage makeup, to disguise himself as an attractive-looking woman. Indeed, Nan Christopher, his twin sister, was sufficient proof of that. Between them was a remarkable resemblance, her features merely a feminine version of his own strong countenance.

With Nan's photograph in front of him, Jimmy set to work— and when he had finished with his make-up kit, and had donned the clothing expert tailors made for him, to all outward appearances it was Nan Christopher who arose from the dressing-ta-

Then the red-clad vandals were amongst the girls, grabbing them!

INVASION FROM THE SKY

ble. In this clever disguise, he rode out past Bartlett with Perley Harbin and stayed with the young farmer. Then Harbin led him through the woods by a roundabout route that took them clear of any possible ambush along the roads leading into the valley.

From that point Operator 5 went on alone, seemingly an alarmed, feminine figure who hugged the cover at the side of the road wherever possible. Past one charred ruin after the other he went, until he reached the path that led to the ash-strewn foundation that was all that remained of Harbin's home. There he turned in, to approach the fire-blackened doorstep slowly, hesitantly, as his eyes flashed around him with pretended apprehension.

His ruse was working! He could fairly feel eyes upon him, watching his every move—and then he caught a glimpse of a huge-headed, red-garbed figure stalking him. Jimmy straightened like a startled deer—and ran frantically toward a thick patch of trees as the creature, aware now that it was discovered, broke from cover.

After him the grotesque pursuer came loping, gaining ground on the short steps Jimmy was forced to simulate. The creature was almost up to its quarry as the trees closed around them—and then suddenly Jimmy was on top of him, his whole fighting weight hurled at the red-garbed body.

Down they went together, and before they hit the ground Jimmy's fingers were tightly fastened in the invader's throat—where the huge helmet met the rubberish uniform. Furiously they threshed and struggled, but Jimmy Christopher was fighting not only for his own existence but for the lives of all America. Tenaciously he clung to that grip.

That fearful struggle seemed to go on forever.... But at last the creature's squirming became less vigorous, its flailing arms grew heavy and lost their strength. At last the globular head stopped tossing, fell back inert—and the invader was dead.

Stripping off the big helmet and tight-fitting uniform, Jimmy got into them himself—and now he was ready. Boldly he stalked out of the trees and walked out to the road—to head straight into the heart of the desolation, resolved to find that rocket-ship or never return!

CHAPTER 6
DEATH TO MISS AMERICA

TO STEM the rising tide of panic now inundating America was almost as important as locating and disposing of the invaders. For, once the great Eastern cities were depopulated, the nation would be hamstrung.

Because of this reason Operator 5 had bent every effort, before leaving Washington, to promote a feeling of normalcy, a reassuring usualness, that would coax the people out of the hysteria that was enveloping them.

"What we have to fight is disorganization," he had told the heads of the public utilities when they answered his hurry-call to arms. "I want the trains to run on schedule, the telephones to operate as usual, the radio to broadcast regularly, light and power to be supplied without interruption. When the usual performance of any of these every-day utilities breaks down it adds immeasurably to the panic. But the very fact that they *are* there, functioning as always, is a reassurance that quiets jittery nerves."

It was true.

To legitimate and motion-picture theater owners, the proprietors of beach resorts—all who supplied public entertainment— he had made a special plea for cooperation.

Among these were members of the Atlantic City Board of Trade.

"The eyes of all America are on Atlantic City at this time of the year," he told them. "Your annual beauty contest is a focus of national attention. I want you to go through with it this year as if *nothing* had happened. The very fact that it is being held as usual will go a long way to restore public confidence and convince people that the danger is not as appalling as they had feared.

"I want you to go through with your plans in order to help me bolster the public morale. But there is also *another* reason for this request, gentlemen. Atlantic City has not yet been touched by the invaders, but your beauty contest may very well bring them. We will be prepared for that. The general staff of the army is working out a trap into which we want the invaders to walk— and we are relying upon you to lead them into it."

"We are willing to do our part," the president of the Board of Trade had promptly agreed, "but I don't know whether or not we *can* stage the show this year. Applications have been coming in very slowly. People are afraid to come near the East. It begins to look as if we will not have more than a handful of contestants. However, you can depend upon us to do our best."

To combat that hesitancy, Jimmy had utilized the radio to spread the word that the beauty contest would be held as usual; used every means of publicity to make the seaside resort appear as carefree and untroubled as ever. But the day after he left for New Hampshire the contest promoters admitted that they were licked. The contest could not be staged.

"We haven't had a dozen entrants—and the contest is only two days off!" the chairman threw up his hands helplessly. "Even those who sent in their applications have canceled them, and most of those who came East to compete have hurried back home. There is nothing to do but call it off."

That was when Diane Elliot rose to her feet and faced him angrily.

"We *can't* call it off," she said flatly. "Operator 5 is depending upon that contest, and we are going to stage it. I will bring you your contestants—as good-looking as you ever have had. From among them you can pick a Miss America who is worthy of the name!"

To keep that boast meant quick work, and Diane lost no time making her preparations. To New York, Philadelphia, Baltimore, Richmond, Atlanta, Jacksonville—to every city within quick reach of the capital her wires speeded. Wires that were addressed to Jimmy Christopher's most dependable agents—and that assigned them a duty far different from any they had ever been called upon to perform....

The next morning the volunteers began to arrive—young, beautiful and shapely, as Diane had specified. But something more than that, besides. The elimination for that contest was the most unusual that had ever been held. Face and figure were important for those girls who passed in review through the little office where Diane sat as sole judge of their fitness. But the courage that was deep in their hearts, the fortitude behind their pretty faces, counted for far more.

The girls who went out of that office with long ribbons which bore the legends *Miss Boston, Miss Los Angeles, Miss Detroit* and the names of more than fifty other cities, had far more purpose than those of other years. They were girls who might have to be depended upon to fight for America; girls who were there, not to win personal glory, but to serve their country—to the death, if necessary....

DIANE WAS with them in the dressing-rooms when it was time to file out before the judges and the assembled thousands. She was clad in a bathing suit herself, prepared to take her place with them in the line. Carefully she watched them as they moved past her, searched their faces for a sign of fear, for a hint of hysteria. But she thrilled with pride at what she saw. In those pretty young faces there was no trace of fright—nothing more than the preliminary nervousness natural to any young girl about to step out before thousands of staring, critical eyes.

Out of that delegation the judges could choose a Miss America of whom the nation could well be proud!

Two-thirds of the contestants had already passed before the judges before Diane took her place in the line. The moment she stepped out into the open pavilion at the edge of the boardwalk her eyes flashed upward to search the sky. It was a clear blue, almost cloudless, with not a shadow on that horizon which might, so suddenly, resolve itself into a threatening air-monster.

Perhaps, after all, this bait that Jimmy had dangled before the eyes of the woman-hungry invaders would not tempt them.

Perhaps the contest would go off without interruption.

Diane turned her eyes back to the pavilion in front of her, where one of the contestants was walking slowly along the runway. Now there were only three others in front of her. Two of these went through the required paces; and Diane got ready, straightened the ribbon that hung suspended from her shoulder, patted her fingers against her chestnut hair to give it a last-minute set—then suddenly the blood in her veins seemed to turn to ice.

There it was—almost on top of them!

Hardly more than a speck in the sky when her upward-turned eyes glimpsed it, the rocket-ship came on with incredible breathtaking speed. Before the wide-eyed girl beside her could recover sufficient control of her fright-palsied vocal muscles to scream, the gleaming air-mammoth streaked in front of them and glided to a standstill on the beach. Instantly its many doors were flung open, the runways dropped into place, and the huge-headed creatures swarmed out upon the sand!

For an instant the thousands of spectators were too completely spellbound to move. Gaping-eyed, they sat there. Then they came to their feet—and a great bellow of insane terror rose into the air as they fought one another desperately in a wild surge toward escape. In a moment's time the peaceful scene had been turned into a mad riot, the laughing crowd into a mob of insensate savages!

Stunning horror overwhelmed Diane as she witnessed that frightful debacle and realized how terribly the plan to trap the invaders had failed. Alert eyes at a score of different points had been scanning the sky tirelessly, watching for that ship. Hidden guns had belched forth a barrage of high-powered explosive shells the moment the monster was spotted—but there had been no provision for such *incredible* speed!

Before the American guns could be discharged, the rocket-ship had altogether upset their range; was right there on top of them, bathing them with a deadly shower of gas and turning the fire-kindling rays upon them. Before a second volley could be fired most of those guns were already ablaze, their doomed crews writhing in flames.

Fiendishly those inhuman butchers turned their gas rays upon the fleeing spectators—to transform them into a roaring bonfire, a field of swaying human wheat touched off by the flames! Cowering in terror, the bathing-suited contestants huddled together—now between the advancing invaders and the furnace that seethed behind them! Then the red-clad creatures were upon them, grabbing them around the waist, by the arms, by the hair—dragging them into that space-devouring leviathan....

THE TRAP had failed utterly! That soul-sickening thought hammered through Diane Elliot's brain as a burly creature bore down on her and seized her arm. Hopelessly she fought him, but he easily lifted her. Helpless as a child, she was borne across the sand and through one of the yawning doorways, into an interior that was much like the corridors of an ocean liner.

Down two flights of stairs he carried her and into a large, barely furnished room that had the appearance of a mess-hall. Here she was turned loose with the other captives—forty or more scantily clad girls who huddled together, sobbing in terror.

Diane hardly dared face those girls and the accusation she must read in their eyes. She was responsible for their presence here. They had trusted her, and she had led them into a trap that would mean their deaths or something far more terrible....

Yet, when they clustered around her, no recrimination showed in their blanched faces. The sight of her here among them helped the stronger ones to soothe and quiet those whose nerves were now close to the breaking point. What horrors awaited them, they dared not visualize—but when the ordeal came they would face it, Diane knew, courageously, heroines as brave as any man who ever walked, unshaken, into the cannon's mouth....

They had not long to wait to learn their fate. In a few minutes the rocket-ship vibrated and tilted slightly upward—and was on its way, God only knew where. Now the dozen guards who had been watching the captives took off their big helmets, squinting at the girls, beady eyes bulging from huge heads. Queer, Mongoloid-looking creatures whose basilisk scrutiny brought shrieks of terror from the trembling prisoners.

Now more than thirty more of the creatures came into the room and unhelmeted as soon as the ship was under way—the fortunate ones who had captured women for themselves, Diane concluded.

Still others arrived—a dozen men who were smaller in stature and had normal size heads. Japanese, she identified them immediately—and realized, at the same instant, that they were the rulers on this ship. The big-headed men made way for them, backed away abjectly while the grinning Japanese looked over the cowering girls and made their choice after an inspection that brought the hot blood surging into the captives' cheeks.

Diane's teeth clenched in her lower lip, and her nails dug deep into the palms of her hands as she endured that insolent inspection. One by one, the girls were seized and dragged, screaming, from the room... and then one of the Japanese stood in front of her. A thick-set little man with a round, flat face and eyes that were mere slits. Evil little eyes that leered at her lasciviously.

"Charming," he murmured in a clipped, mechanical-sounding voice, as he bowed mockingly. "The others—they have no eyes. I apologize for them. You will do Mabuchi the honor?"

His arm was held for her. Diane scorned it, but when his fingers clenched in her arm she made no attempt to resist him. Smiling widely, he led her from the room and down another flight of stairs to a smaller compartment that, she saw at once, was his private cabin.

Mabuchi's smile widened when he turned the key in his lock and turned to confront her, when he advanced toward her confidently and reached out to grasp the shoulder-strap of her bathing suit—but his assurance faded surprisingly when he was suddenly pulled forward and sent sprawling on the back of his neck at the other side of the cabin. Deprived of the mask of that mocking grin, his features became cruel and hard, his narrow eyes the murderous slits of a stalking panther.

"So you have been taught ju-jitsu?" he purred. "Then you will interested in broadening your knowledge of the science. You will, no doubt, appreciate the artistry of *this*—"

With a lithe leap he was across the cabin, snatching at her wrist, his snaky eyes gloating with anticipation. But Diane did not dare to trust her knowledge of the Japanese defense art against this fellow who, for all she knew, might be one of its masters. Desperately her eyes darted around the cabin, seeking a weapon, anything to hold him off if only for a few seconds until she could plan how to cope with him.

There was nothing. Nothing but one of those globular metal helmets on top of his dresser.

In a bound she had reached it, had seized it and hurled it straight at his head. Her aim was good. The helmet slammed against his forehead, despite his effort to ward it off. It knocked him back, sent him reeling against the wall as the helmet crashed to the floor.

Mabuchi was on his feet again in an instant—to be met by the overturning center table, which up-ended against his shins and then came down on his toes. Before he could get out from behind it, Diane had him by the shoulders, pulled him headlong over it and sprawled him on his face on the floor. Springing over him, she ran to the door and turned the key, yanked it open— only to run squarely into the arms of a man who held her tightly and pinned her helplessly against his chest!

THE NEWCOMER was an older man than Mabuchi; a

91

heavy-set man in his late forties, Diane judged him. He was partially bald and wore horn-rimmed glasses that magnified his eyes startlingly. Cold, crafty eyes that were filled with satirical amusement as he stared down at Mabuchi. "I hope I have not intruded?" he chuckled, as he made a pretended attempt to withdraw. "Or perhaps you would not mind having an old man watch your—er, gymnastic technique with the ladies, Mabuchi?"

"Your Excellence is welcome to the poor comforts of this humble cabin at any time."

Without loosening his tight hold on Diane, his "Excellence" stepped inside.

"I am afraid you have made a mistake, Mabuchi," his voice was silky, taunting. "It is not wise to unloose a tigress in your little cabin—unless you have had more experience handling one of that sort. My quarters are much better equipped for entertaining this young lady."

"It is an honor that Rai Kasuga-Tosa should see fit to approve my humble taste," Mabuchi parroted stonily. "It is a privilege to be able to offer the woman to your Excellence."

"Thank you, Mabuchi," Kasuga-Tosa half-bowed.

His lean, hard fingers closed like a vise on Diane's wrist as he made her a mock-obeisance and propelled her out into the corridor. Without a word he led the way to a door that opened onto a private staircase, down that and into a suite of rooms that were rich in a lavish display of luxurious furnishings. The moment he appeared, bowing servants seemed to materialize from every corner.

"I am taking a new member into my household," he told them

briefly. "Take her inside and see that she is properly clothed to greet me on my return."

The servants closed in on Diane and fairly swept her into a large, richly decorated room, where more than a dozen girls—white girls, American girls!—sat cross-legged on pillows or sprawled at full length on rich, soft rugs and low divans. Girls who roused themselves from their apathy to start at her as she was led past them and into a smaller room where an ancient Japanese crone took her in charge.

Under the old woman's sign-language direction she stripped off her bathing suit and put on soft, silken garments that clung to her figure even more revealingly than the scanty one-piece. Then, it seemed, she was free to return to the big room—Kasuga-Tosa's harem.

Immediately she was surrounded by the girls, who had been expectantly watching the doorway. Girls with stricken faces, with eyes so filled with hopelessness that it hurt to look into them. "You must be Bea Halliday," Diane hazarded when one of them identified herself as a member of the "Tomorrow and Forever" company that had been playing in New York. "Herbert Carrol came to Washington to report your abduction."

But the girl was shaking her head. "I am not Bea Halliday," she said softly. "Bea isn't here any longer. She tried to kill Kasuga-Tosa. Did you notice those deep scratches on his neck? She did that—and before she died every inch of skin on her body had been scratched off with devilish claws and barbs.

"Yes, at present we are the 'favorites' of the commander," she said bitterly, as she saw the surprised question in Diane's eyes,

"But his Excellence is notoriously fickle. His moods change from hour to hour—and when one of us no longer fits into his mood she becomes a plaything for those big-headed barbarians. They are beasts, those creatures. Sometimes their playthings live for days. The *lucky* ones are torn to pieces in a few hours—"

"And the commander allows them—to do that?" Diane gasped.

"*Allows* them?" came the incredulous answer. "He watches them and eggs them on to more beastly excesses."

That was Kasuga-Tosa, the man who was beating America to her knees with his barbarous killers and his invincible weapons! A ruthless sadist, who tortured and murdered for the sheer delight of watching human suffering; who spread wanton destruction simply to appease his hellish appetite. America had faced the threat of many ruthless dictators—but never the certain doom that now hung over every man, woman and child if this unholy monster was not defeated.

"Surely, there must be some way of killing—of *executing*—such a beast!" Diane said tensely. "Surely, you can overpower him—all of you together. One rush when he least expects it—"

"And the moment we made the first move his guards would be on top of us," one of them shrugged hopelessly. "Others have tried that. They are no longer with us. It's useless—"

"But it isn't!" Diane insisted. "It can't be! If you no longer care what happens to you, you must think of the millions of other women whose fate depends upon you. If we let this beast over-run America, they will *all* be doomed. You can't let America down like that."

94

"No," the silky voice of Kasuga-Tosa seemed to be right at her ear, and Diane saw him stepping out from behind a silken drapery that had seemed to be part of the solid wall. "They really can't do that. You will have to coach them in their role of patriotic martyrs—but a little later, pretty one, a little later."

Again his fingers fastened like steel hooks in her arm, and she was drawn across the big room to another silken drapery that parted as he stepped through it—parted and revealed a door that opened into a sybaritic bed-chamber. Again the door latched behind her, and Diane made a swift, desperate inventory of the room's contents.

Nothing that could help her! Nothing that she could use as a weapon! Every article in this room was soft and downy, soft and voluptuous—pillows and cushions, deep-pile rugs, divans that were not higher than a foot from the floor. Not even a chair that she might grab and wield as a flail, as a threat to hold him off.

She was at this monster's mercy—but somehow she must get away from him; must get out into the main part of this hell-ship and gain control of it. Somehow, she must destroy it with all its evil company. This was America's only hope....

Diane tensed, watched him coming toward her with what he intended to be disarming unconcern. Every nerve atingle, every muscle flexed—and then she darted at him, desperately trusting again to the ju-jitsu that seemed to be her only weapon. Her hands secured their hold, tightened in one of the surest grips Jimmy Christopher had taught her—only to have it broken, to have her arms twisted until it seemed that they must pop from their shoulder sockets.

Helplessly her face turned up to Kasuga-Tosa's.

"One of the finest grips taught by the master, Kashawatska Hoia," he admitted, his face almost against hers; "but unfortunately it seems you do not know its counter-grip."

His eyes were burning down at her, mocking her; the pressure became more cruel, more unbearable. Beads of perspiration stood out on her forehead. Her last defense had failed—but no, no! There was still one other!

Diane gasped, and her head fell back limply. Suddenly she was limp and unresisting in his arms, sank lifelessly to the floor when he lowered her. Kasuga-Tosa bent over her curiously— and like a flash she bounded up to a sitting position, the top of her head smashing into his teeth! The Jap gasped, cursed as he reeled backward and went down—but Diane was after him like a savage beast driven berserk by hunger.

Kasuga-Tosa was half-stunned. Struggling to get to his knees and at the same time back away from her, he tried to protect his eyes by covering his face with his arms.

That was the chance Diane had been seeking. Suddenly she leaped to her feet and sprang to the door. Frantically she grasped the latch and turned it. The moment her hand closed over the knob, the door opened—and in surged a throng of men. Men?

Diane stared at them, stared at one face that *could* not be there among them, and then her heart seemed to sink right through her breast....

CHAPTER 7
LEVIATHAN OF THE AIR

WHEN JIMMY CHRISTOPHER headed into the wilderness that lay beyond Perley Harbin's valley, his own plans were chaotic. Somewhere ahead of him, he was convinced, lay the hideout of the rocket-ship, but how he would find it when the best of local guides had failed he did not know. Perhaps if he met another of the invaders he might overcome the fellow and force him to act as a guide—or he might stay in the background and follow the creature back to the ship....

The man he had killed had carried no ray-projector, but in a cleverly concealed side-pocket of the overall covering Jimmy found a fully loaded automatic. With the two of his own he already carried, that equipped him with quite an arsenal. Yet bullets would be of no real use against these creatures; he must depend on the weapon of *surprise.*

Alertly he watched both sides of the now almost indistinguishable road, as he penetrated deeper into the wilderness. Then almost as if it had dropped from the sky, one of the invaders suddenly materialized beside him. Jimmy returned the creature's stare, though he could not see beyond the round goggle-eyes that were opaque from the outside. At least the fellow could not see his face, either—or that he was an impostor.

But now his companion was making signs with his hands—attempting to communicate with him in some sort of manual code. When Jimmy pretended not to see it, the other tugged at his arm and repeated his message—and then there was no avoiding the issue.

Jimmy thought fast. Suddenly his foot stubbed against a tree root that extended out into the path. He stumbled, reached out to grab something for support—and then his arms closed around his companion, bore him to the ground. Surprise was his only advantage in the grim battle that followed. The invader was a bigger and more powerful man than he. Jimmy came down on top of him, dived for that deadly throat grip before the fellow knew just what had happened. After that it was either man's fight. Twice the burly invader got to his feet and almost broke that tenacious grip on his throat. But Jimmy bore him down again and endured the merciless battering of his ribs and midriff, as he squeezed, inexorably. Panting for breath in that metal helmet, his senses swam... but it was his burly opponent who finally sank back, limply.

Jimmy had won, but he knew that he could not emerge victorious in another such battle. So much strength had gone out of him that he was barely able to drag the inert body into the bushes, and then continue his pilgrimage into *nowhere*....

The huge helmet was a protection for his head in a struggle such as the one through which he had just come, but it was a handicap. Now his ears were of no assistance; he had to depend entirely upon his eyes to warn him of danger—and they almost failed him. Breasting a little rise in the trail, he rounded a thick clump of tangled undergrowth and almost walked into two of the huge-headed creatures who were just arising from where they had been lying on the ground.

Just in time he flung himself back, crawled into the brush and waited there tensely, to ascertain whether or not they had seen him. They had *not!* Without a glance in his direction, they turned and pressed on into the wilderness—with Jimmy now close on their heels.

At times the way was almost impenetrable, no longer even a discernible trail, but at last it opened into a wild valley deep in the hills. A valley that was ceilinged over by a tremendous, spider-web-like net that seemed to extend for miles!

JIMMY STARED up at it in amazement. Made of some thin, gossamer material, it hardly obstructed the rays of the sun, filtering the light down greenishly into a wide, flat bottom, where three great rocket-ships lay moored! Here was the hideout—and that great net was the reason it had not been spotted from the air. Spanning the valley from side to side, it furnished a perfect camouflage against the most powerful glasses that might be trained upon it from above.

Almost inaccessible by foot, and safely concealed from aerial observation, this hiding-place might have defied the efforts of thousands of searchers for months... yes, for years! But now Operator 5 stood on its brink—and debated the desperate decision he must make.

To go back and return with reinforcements—or to go on into that valley alone, trusting to his disguise to take him to the nearest of the ships and give him an opportunity to capture or wreck it.... He had found the hideout, he reasoned swiftly, but even if he managed to get back to Bartlett without being discovered he could not possibly hope to lead an adequate force of men through the wilderness he had traversed—and it would be equally hopeless, trying to locate that valley from the air. Even though he knew how it was concealed, its protective camouflage would baffle him as completely as it had before he knew of its existence.

To return was out of the question. There was no alternative but to go ahead and tackle that host single-handed!

Now Jimmy's unsuspecting guides were out of sight, lost among nearly a hundred of their fellows who came and went from the ships. Two of those ships, farther back in the valley, were more or less neglected, but the largest of the three—the one nearest to him—seemed to be the center of activity. From the way the big-headed creatures were bustling around it, Jimmy got the impression that it had very recently landed… although he had seen no sign of it in the sky.

This ship, he decided, would be his goal. Making certain that the way was clear behind him, he stepped out into the path and headed toward it. Several of the invaders went by him on the valley floor but paid him no attention. Not even when he was right down among them was his presence noticed.

So far so good. Now to enter the ship without arousing suspicion. A dozen or more doors were open, but he had noticed that most of those who were entering or leaving the craft used the doors on the second tier from the bottom. He headed for one of those, walked up the runway—and had to press to one side to make way for two men who were coming from it.

Jimmy's nerves tensed as the fellows brushed past him. He could fairly feel their eyes boring into him—and when he reached the doorway and was able to cast a look back he saw that he had not imagined their scrutiny. They had stopped—were looking back at him!

That meant that he had no time to lose. They were suspicious, might return to the ship to question him—and there was no hope of disposing of them as he had handled the fellow on the trail. Jimmy stepped through the doorway into a metal-walled corridor that was lined with closed doors. As quickly as he dared, he strode along it until he reached a short cross-corridor that was the landing for stairs going up and down.

Which way? *Up*, Jimmy decided quickly. That ought to be the direction of the control-rooms—and there was the most likely place to find the commander of the expedition.

Two flights of stairs he climbed before he reached the topmost corridor and started toward the front of the ship. It seemed to be deserted up there—not a soul to be seen—until he almost collided with a silk-jacketed servant. A Japanese! The fellow stared at him in surprise, but Jimmy did not wait. He hurried forward to where the corridor terminated in a wide room that was lit by daylight. The control-room!

AT THE doorway he hesitated. There were four men inside—not the usual, big-headed creatures. But short, squat Japanese. They wore blue silken uniforms instead of the red coveralls and helmets. If he could overpower them, could get control of that cabin and hold it against the rest of the ship, he might force them to take the craft up into the air. He might even be able to force them to pilot it to Washington and turn it over to the army aeronautical experts!

Quietly Jimmy stepped inside and unfastened the hooked-back doors, closed them silently and fumbled with the latch that would secure them—but at that moment the handicap of his sound-muffling helmet was his undoing. Suddenly the doors were flung inward and he was knocked backward as the Japanese servant and two officers rushed in, followed by a dozen red-garbed creatures!

One of Jimmy's automatics was in his hand, even as he went down. From the floor he accounted for two of the Japanese and triggered a shot at a third—but then the big-headed men were on top of him. Four of them leaped upon him and pinned him down helplessly, while others wrested the gun from his fingers.

Unable to move an arm or leg, he lay pinioned there while they unfastened his helmet and removed it. Even through those masking helmets, he could glimpse their amazement as they looked down at this stranger who should have been one of themselves.

But the Japanese officers who stood over him lost no time in amazement. Their slant eyes widened and then were slitted again. One barked an order at the big-headed men in a language Jimmy had never heard. Quickly the creatures pulled him to his feet, closed around him, and marched him out after the officers.

That procession moved back to the stairway by which he had come, but instead of stopping at the landing where he had entered the ship, it went on down, three floors lower—and into an amazing room that looked like the harem of an Oriental potentate! A harem populated with frightened-faced American girls!

Through it he was swept, and up to a door that opened the moment the leader touched it—opened to reveal Diane Elliot, clad in flowing Japanese robes, in the doorway! Diane, her eyes wide, her face suddenly ashen-pale as she caught sight of him.

"Jimmy!" she gasped. "Jimmy!" And then her hand flew to her mouth, as if to jam the syllables back into her throat.

Not until then did Jimmy see the man who was picking himself up from amidst a pile of cushions. His face was scratched and bleeding, his silken uniform torn, and in one hand he held the shattered remnant of his horn-rimmed spectacles. Kasuga-Tosa's face was flushed with rage as he shot a venomous glance first at Diane and then at Jimmy.

One of the Japanese started to speak, to explain how they had caught this American masquerading in a uniform and a helmet. But the raging commander cut him short.

" 'Jimmy,' you call him?" he snarled as he came close and peered into the prisoner's face. "Jimmy—but I call him Operator 5! You see, I am not altogether unfamiliar with this country over which I shall soon rule. I know you well, Operator 5. I am delighted that you have come here—especially at such a well timed moment. Take him outside—into the big room," he snapped in Japanese. Then, "Get rid of the others—they are no longer needed. We will handle this ourselves."

Like fascinating snakes his eyes darted back to Jimmy Christopher; eyes that barely peered through his narrowed lids, until a servant brought another pair of glasses. "There are others here who will appreciate watching us extend to you our Japa-

Infuriated at last, the girls charged the Japanese!

nese hospitality," he explained, with a grin that barely curled his hard mouth.

IN THE outer room the huge-headed men were dismissed, their places taken by servants who gripped Jimmy's arms securely and dragged him to a point opposite where Kasuga-Tosa had seated himself on a low, dais-like couch, the frightened girls crouching and lying in a semicircle at his feet.

"Operator 5—and she calls him 'Jimmy?'" Kasuga-Tosa's voice was soft, sibilant, as if he was talking to himself. "Then perhaps this one is best fitted to furnish entertainment for our guest. *This one!*" he nodded at Diane—and two brawny servants seized her.

Dragging her up onto his low platform, they forced her to her knees, bent her head forward and ripped the silken garments from her back. Like a devil-priest the goggle-eyed commander loomed above her and with slow deliberation drew a long, thin-bladed dagger from a belt-sheath.

"Lovely skin," he half-whispered, as he ran his fingers over the back of her neck. "It would be too bad to let it perish. Better to save it—to preserve it for future generations. I shall be very careful so as to damage it as little as possible."

As he spoke, the needle point pricked the skin at the back of her neck, started downward in a thin, red line. *He was going to skin Diane alive!*

Jimmy stared with burning eyes. Frantically he fought to free himself. But his captors were prepared for that; they held his arms back so that he could scarcely move. Bitter curses tore from his lips—and Kasuga-Tosa only seemed to become more absorbed in his devilish work.

The razor-edged knife traveled slowly, downward… then suddenly it stopped, while the Japanese looked up in annoyed surprise.

One of the girls, a few yards away, had risen to her feet, was glaring at him with blazing eyes.

"Stop!" she screamed. "Stop it—you bloody butcher! You cowardly murderer of unborn babies! You have done enough—"

Like a missile suddenly released from a catapult, she flung herself at him. Barehanded, she clutched him, buried her face against his—then sank her teeth into his throat!

Kasuga-Tosa screamed as he tried to back away, but her arms were wound around him in a grip that only death would break. His dagger rose and fell, stabbed her back, shoulders, neck, bathing her with blood—but he could not cast her off. Together they fell to the floor… and then the servants came to their senses.

Rushing to his aid, they grabbed hold of the girl and tried to drag her away—only to find ten more girls tearing and clawing wildly at their faces, their eyes, their hair; ten girls who had been cowering helplessly a moment before and now were transformed into savage Amazons.

Jimmy Christopher was forgotten in that hectic moment. His captors dropped him and ran to the assistance of their fellows. For an instant he hesitated, about to throw himself into the mêlée. But one of the girls was at his side, had him by the sleeve, was holding him back.

"No—no, Operator 5!" she begged. "You can do nothing

there! Get away while there is time—it's America's only hope!"
Now she had Diane by the hand, was dragging her toward the
door. "I can get you away safely—if only there is time!"

The great-headed men had deprived Jimmy of one of his
guns, the automatic he had taken from their dead mate. But
they had not found the two he had hidden in his clothing. Now
these were in his hands. One he clutched, ready for action. The
other he thrust into the hand of his volunteer guide. Now she
led the way through the doorway out into the corridor. Then
Jimmy vaulted past her, leaped upon a Japanese who had been
crouching there, eavesdropping on the commander who had
taken away his woman. That Japanese was Ito Mabuchi.

Jimmy's automatic was in his back in a moment.

"You're coming with us!" he snapped, booting the other in
front of him. "Move fast—unless you want to feel this gun-bar-
rel over your skull!"

Mabuchi's dark eyes gleamed out of a face that was twisted
into a mask of hatred, but he lost no time obeying. The girl
led the way toward the rear of the ship, her eyes flashing back
anxiously to see if they were being pursued.

"We were going to attack him tonight," she panted to Diane,
as they hurried on. "After he took you in there, we decided to
strike no matter what became of us. But when everything started
to happen, and we saw what he was going to do to you, Thelma
couldn't hold back any longer. Poor Thelma... but at least
she won't suffer now." Thelma—that was the name of Perley
Harbin's sister-in-law.... Now Jimmy understood that tortured
cry of "unborn-baby killer" she had hurled at Kasuga-Tosa. His

jaws clenched so tightly that they ached. Kasuga-Tosa was still alive; was so strongly guarded in that hell-ship that it would be suicide now to attempt to reach him. But he would pay for those barbarous atrocities and beastly indignities he had heaped upon defenseless American women....

NOW THE girl was leading the way down a short flight of steps and into a large chamber where two peculiar craft, that looked like great silver bullets, were parked. About eight feet high and nearly twenty feet long, the front of each came to a rounded point, the upper half of the sloping sides studded with narrow, slotlike windows. In the rear were three rings of heavy metal pipes, each about a foot in diameter, their open ends forming a funnel around a larger open cylinder that was its center.

"You can get away in one of these," she panted. "The back of the ship opens automatically when you—"

Her voice faltered and panic filled her eyes as the corridor they had just quitted reverberated with the sound of angry shouts and running feet. The pursuers were right here, on their heels—coming through the doorway, leaping down the steps. But the girl was tugging frantically at the door of the curious bullet-ship, had gotten it open and was holding it wide while Diane clambered inside.

"Now you," Jimmy commanded, and pushed her inside when she tried to draw back and stand beside him as he blasted three shots at the foremost of the Japanese. "And *you*," to Mabuchi. "Inside there and get to work at those controls."

His free hand was twisted in the fellow's collar, forcing him to the door, thrusting him inside. But now the Japanese were milling all around the door. Jimmy clubbed out at them with his weapon, then reeled back as a bludgeon thudded down on his shoulder. He saw it raised to strike again. Then a bullet drilled a hole in the assailant's temple, as an automatic suddenly barked from the doorway of the ship.

That checked the enemy, momentarily. Jimmy stepped half way through the door—and suddenly the girl came plummeting out; flung herself directly in front of him and took in her own body the hail of bullets that would have cut him down. She died even before she dropped to the floor, before Jimmy was able to slam the door closed. But in that split-second he glimpsed her face and saw that a half-smile was on her lips....

Who she was he did not know. But in his memory she would always be the Unknown Heroine, the girl who had yielded her life as heroically as any man, not for Operator 5 but for her country—the America for whom she wanted him to live and serve....

Once the door was closed, and Jimmy's gun pressed against the back of his neck, Mabuchi lost all his hostility. Docilely he bent over the controls, and in a moment the rear wall of the rocket-ship raised from the floor and slid upward until it was out of sight. With a tremendous roar, the silver bullet sped out of the opening like a shell leaving the mouth of a cannon. In a steep arc it zoomed upward, clearing the tops of the trees and leaving the ground behind so fast that the earth now seemed to disappear magically.

IN THE seat behind Mabuchi, Jimmy leaned over and looked down. The terrain far below was now an indistinct blur. Such speed was incredible, but it was no doubt the reason why the rocket-ship had been able to operate even in daylight without its hideout being discovered. With such speed the ship would be no more than a flash overhead, a speck high in the sky that was gone before anyone had time to take note of it.

And with that speed it would fairly eat up distance, span the entire breadth of the United States in an hour or two! Jimmy leaned over Mabuchi's shoulder, and his automatic muzzle pressed close.

"We are going to Washington," he ordered. "I want to land as close as possible to the burned Capitol building."

"I can come down in the middle of Constitution Plaza," Mabuchi answered sullenly... and presently they were gliding to a landing amid the blackened ruins of the square that had been America's pride.

The appearance of that strange visitor from the sky threw the jittery capital into a panic. Sirens screamed their warning, and the frightened populace scrambled to the bomb-proof shelters with which all the main streets had been equipped. Abruptly Washington had taken on the appearance of a deserted city. But Jimmy knew where he would find men who remained at their posts no matter what alarm might rout their fellow-men.

As he expected, King and his associates had not left their quarters. They were in the midst of an experiment, and working with them were Herbert Carrol and Myron Sumner. King opened the door.

"We've got it, Operator 5!" he enthused. "We've found something that will resist their inflammable gas! Silicate-steel! We are already producing it in half a dozen mills—turning it out in sheets of armor-plate. And now we are trying to incorporate the silicate in a composition cloth that can be used for coverall uniforms. It is the carbon that this gas mixes with to ignite when the rays are projected upon it. We can eliminate that danger by substituting silicate."

It was with difficulty that Jimmy stemmed his jubilant outburst.

Like children presented with a new and fascinating toy, King and his assistants crowded around the tiny rocket-ship and examined it minutely. In their absorption they questioned Mabuchi as if he were one of them—and strangely he answered in the same manner. He willingly demonstrated the ship's operation, showed them how to manipulate the controls.

It was not until Jimmy had taken him to his office for questioning that he began to understand Mabuchi's surprising transformation.

"I am free now—I can say what I like. While I was on the space-ship I could say nothing, I could do nothing—not unless it pleased the Honorable Rai Kasuga-Tosa to give me his most gracious permission.

"He was master of my waking and my sleeping for too long," he spat out. "It is good to be away from him. But I want to see him again, Mr. Operator 5. Very much I want to see him again. There are certain matters between his Excellence and me that still remain to be adjusted—and perhaps you will permit me to start that adjustment by offering you my services in any sort of capacity you may desire."

MYRON SUMNER was one of that little group in Operator

112

5's office. He had been watching Mabuchi keenly, and now he impulsively took the questioning out of Jimmy's hands.

"You are a Japanese, of course, Mabuchi?" he asked.

Mabuchi nodded confirmation.

"And these big-headed men—who are they?" Sumner followed up.

"They are members of a lost tribe my countrymen discovered during the pacification of China," Mabuchi answered readily. "They lived in a series of valleys in Western China, close to Tibet—a section that was entirely cut off from the rest of the world. Apparently they had been closed up there for centuries, having no contact with anyone outside the hills that shut them in and shut others out.

"Their civilization had degenerated in most respects, but they seem to have retained the secrets of the inflammable gas and the ray-projector that must have come down to them from their forefathers. Perhaps that is why they were able to maintain their isolation. We lost thousands of men before these people were conquered, and then we were able to accomplish that only by exterminating most of them. The survivors were taken to Japan and are now serving as vassals, as you saw."

"Then the Japanese government is behind this unprovoked attack upon the United States?" Jimmy interposed quickly.

"Rai Kasuga-Tosa is a nobleman of Japan and his officers are at present on leave from the Japanese army," Mabuchi replied, and a bland grin spread over his face. "But, of course, the Japanese government would promptly disavow any knowledge of them or any responsibility for them. That you will understand."

113

Jimmy Christopher understood all too well.

"These rocket-ships—they are Japanese?" he questioned, although the words were more a statement than a query.

"Japan has made tremendous strides in aviation that the rest of the world little suspects," Mabuchi answered. "This expedition affords an excellent opportunity for our observers to watch their creations in actual operation. I am an aeronautical engineer. My specialty was the little emergency rocket-ship which you gentlemen have just inspected. That is why I was with Kasuga-Tosa."

Yes, Jimmy understood completely. Imperial Japan was the power behind this piratical invasion—but the hand of the Mikado was well concealed. Utilizing these strange and unknown tribesmen for the physical performance of the onslaught, no responsibility could be traced to Nippon in the event that any of them were killed or captured. Only the officers, who stayed safely within the protection of the ships, were Japanese—and even they would swear that theirs was a private expedition, without the sanction of their government.

Safely cloaked by this shallow pretense, the Japanese war lords were using America as a testing ground for their infernal destruction engines; a second China, to be torn and ravaged by war and then enslaved when a puppet state was set up within its borders....

Myron Sumner had been thinking, too. Jimmy recognized that remote, abstracted look in the depths of his eyes—and now Sumner spoke.

"We have one of the rocket-ships and a man who is expert in their construction," he said significantly. "Looks to me like a break for our side. We can put those ships into production immediately—if Mr. Mabuchi will draw up the plans for us. I am in favor of accepting his offer and enlisting him as a technical adviser to help us build a defense fleet."

"Not a defense fleet," Jimmy corrected him. "We want an *offense* fleet. With this little emergency ship as a model, we must build super-rocket-ships—craft so powerful that they can engage and obliterate Kasuga-Tosa's trio of destroyers!"

And Ito Mabuchi nodded his head in vigorous endorsement. "That can be done," he confirmed.

Operator 5 set that program under way at once. By morning the big airplane factories at Schenectady were being reorganized for their new task, carloads of material were speeding to them, and the best aeronautical experts in America, with Mabuchi at their side, were at work upon the new plans Jimmy had demanded.

That work progressed swiftly—but meanwhile Kasuga-Tosa was not idle. The rocket-ships were lashing out savagely. New London, Fall River, Worcester, Brockton—a dozen cities in stricken New England were swept by death and left in smoldering ruins. Jimmy came away from those scenes of wanton destruction with a heavy heart. But, at last, he consoled himself, he had his hands upon a weapon that would enable America to defeat these barbarous invaders; would enable her to wipe them from the face of the earth!

CHAPTER 8
THEY SHALL NOT PASS!

BUT TO build those super rocket-ships, even after the plans were perfected, would take time—and Kasuga-Tosa almost seemed to sense the preparations that were being made against him. He pushed his advantage, inexorably. Within another week all of industrial New England had been laid waste and the destruction was spreading steadily, like a poisonous cancer, toward New York.

Desperately, Operator 5 and the army chiefs rallied their forces on the west bank of the Connecticut River and tried to stem the invasion there. But Kasuga-Tosa's big-headed minions swept on irresistibly. Advancing in front of the rocket-ships, they scourged the entire countryside; desolated it as if a plague of locusts had attacked it.

Regiment after regiment, division after division tried to make a stand against them and were routed, their ranks decimated by a fiery doom against which they had no adequate protection.

"It is sheer murder asking men to stand up against those flames," General Daniel Logan protested, as the scorched remnants of his shattered divisions streamed across Vermont. "It's like condemning them to death at the stake! We can't stop these monsters no matter how we try."

But the invaders *had* to be stopped or, at least slowed up—to gain as much time as possible for those factories now working day and night in Schenectady.

"We *must* stop them," Jimmy Christopher muttered grimly,

as he ordered up fresh troops to check the rout and attempt a stand in the passes of the Green Mountains.

Those new troops had the partial protection of screens made of the new flameproof armor-plate, but they had little chance against the superior arms of the invaders. The big-headed creatures crept up on them, ferreted into positions from which their ray-projectors would reach behind the screens—and again fiery death ran rampant. Again the precipitate retreat became a disorganized rout. Across Lake Champlain the fleeing survivors poured.

With haggard eyes Operator 5 stared down at the military map spread out before him, gauging the distance to Schenectady. Scarcely more than a hundred miles remained. Already he had thrown his every resource, his every reserve, between Kasuga-Tosa and those all-important factories—and everything had been swept away by the all-consuming flames. But the invaders *had* to be held back! He had been fighting to gain days of respite; now every hour that he could hold them off was invaluable. Little more than a hundred miles of open country—and Kasuga-Tosa would walk into the factories that were to have doomed him; would wipe out the nearly completed rocket-ships even before they were launched....

Flat, open country, once the invaders were past the lakes—but there, at the foot of Lake Champlain, was a spot where they might be halted; might be held at least for a few hours. Fort Ticonderoga! When America was new-born that rocky height had been one of her bulwarks of defense. Perhaps now, nearly

117

two centuries later, the Revolutionary monument could again be enlisted for the defense of the nation!

The fort, Jimmy knew, was in good condition. It had been restored to much of its original appearance and strength, and the old cannon were still there at the ports in the walls. Heavy guns were of utmost importance if the invaders were to be stopped, and the American forces had been practically stripped of their artillery. Most of the heavy field-pieces had been burned to ashes where they stood; the rest had been abandoned when the guncrews fled, precipitately.

Powder and shot could be rushed to Ticonderoga—Jimmy planned it swiftly. Truckloads of armor-plate could be speeded there also; could be fastened to the front of the fort and rigged up overhead as a protection against ray-projectors operated from the little auxiliary rocket-ships. The plan would work—if only he could get the men!

"Do what you can to rally the troops you encounter," he quickly instructed General Logan and the members of his staff. "Lead as many as you can to Ticonderoga. I'll meet you there with enough volunteers to hold the fort."

Swiftly he set to work, phoning and telegraphing his orders; arranging for the shipment of the necessary supplies. Then he turned to his second necessity—men. Mounted on a motorcycle, he roared through Port Henry, Burdick, Crown Point, Chilson, Streetroad, Baldwin—every village within a twenty-mile radius of the fort. At every farmhouse, every tavern, every store, he stopped—and when his machine sputtered on its way again,

119

grim-faced men made preparations to follow him. Men, and their women, too.

Into the old fort they streamed, an army without uniforms, armed with rifles and shotguns, with every conceivable weapon that had come to hand; an army ready to battle to the death for their homes and the liberties their forefathers had won for them in this very stronghold. Within twenty-four hours Ticonderoga was garrisoned to capacity, the old cannon had been cleaned and made ready, the new armor-plate protection had been riveted in place—and watchful eyes were searching the sky for a sign of the invaders.

THEY HAD not long to wait. With startling suddenness the rocket-ships made their appearance, circled overhead, and then swooped down to disembark their horde on the shore below. From three sides the attackers closed in, while the small, silver-bullet ships hovered overhead like venomous insects, seeking a chance to penetrate the armor-plate defenses with their firebrand rays.

With the first charge, the old guns behind those armored parapets poured forth a steady rain of missiles. Big round cannonballs that sought the ships, volley after volley of shrapnel that hurled back the big-headed climbers who bobbed through the brush like strange apparitions from a fantastic, nightmare world.

Jimmy Christopher was everywhere in that rejuvenated fort, cheering and encouraging the sweating men at the guns, directing the distribution of the ammunition; alert and watchful always to see that the defenses were not in danger of being breached.

In the rush of ordering supplies he had overlooked one thing. It rose to plague him the moment the gunners made ready their pieces. It was the wadding. He had forgotten that those old muzzle-loading cannon needed wadding. When the oversight was discovered, it was already too late. No truck would dare run the deadly gauntlet of those hovering rocket-ships that had now put Ticonderoga under siege.

The gunners promptly solved that problem. They tore up their coats and shirts and stuffed them in the gun-muzzles; their undershirts, everything but their trousers—until they stood there, barefooted and naked to the waist, like naval gunners on the old frigates.

But even that stock of wadding soon ran out. The gunners looked around in vain for more, and then stood helpless beside their useless guns. Piece after piece went out of commission—until Diane Elliot, coming up with a wheelbarrow-load of powder, saw what was happening. For an instant, she hesitated—then suddenly stripped off her blouse and skirt, and handed them to one of the gunners. Startled feminine eyes widened, cheeks flushed, yet, one by one, the women silently followed her example. The silenced guns went back into commission, blasting their loads of iron and steel at the enemy—and constantly demanding more wadding to tamp down the charges. Article after article of feminine apparel they consumed… until the toiling women wore little more than the men.

False modesty had lost its significance in that grave emergency. Nothing mattered now but keeping those guns in commission. Nothing was important save driving back the murderous invaders and gaining time—precious minutes and hours for those other toilers in the factories miles behind this desperately resisting outpost.

Operator 5 silently gave thanks in that moment for American women—and for American men. For, as he passed from gun-port to gun-port, he saw that not a man turned his eyes from his task. None gave the slightest indication that he was aware of the near-nakedness now all around him....

For hours that furious battle raged. Twice the invaders reached the walls and had to be hurled down in hand-to-hand fighting. The hovering rocket-ships bathed the defenders with gas that converted them into potential firebrands. But even when their clothing burst into flame, those embattled patriots remembered the sacred cause for which they fought—and flung themselves headlong over the steep cliff rather than drop back behind the barricades and spread the blaze among their fellows.

Kasuga-Tosa's slaves were no match for such courage. Again and again the American guns blasted them away from the fortifications—and at last Jimmy thrilled to the sound of the ear-piercing whistle he had come to know so well. The Japanese was sounding the recall—ordering his defeated tribesmen back into the ships!

"They're quitting!" one of the gunners yelled. "They're licked! We've won! We've won!"

Unbelievingly, the others peered out over the edge of the ramparts and then clambered out, to shout their delirious defiance and hug one another in a mad dance of victory, while the air rang with the cheers of their comrades. At last the invaders had been repulsed, had been made to turn back… if only for a few hours. The effect of that victory was intoxicating. Jimmy Christopher turned from watching the rocket-ships depart to observe the new elation and confidence, that now stirred his gallant company. This enthusiasm would be contagious. It would sweep out over the country and do much to quiet the panic, would rally the discouraged troops and unite the nation for a new, determined defense that would not abate until the last invader had been killed or driven from American soil.…

This was what Jimmy Christopher fondly thought—but at that very moment Tim Donovan was speeding toward Ticonderoga with news calculated to shatter that hopeful dream!

TIM DONOVAN was weary. He had worked more than ten hours that day in the office of the Schenectady airplane plant where the new super-rocket-ships were being manufactured, yet now, at ten-thirty tonight, somehow he could not sleep, could not rest quietly in the little furnished room where he was quartered. The big plant was running twenty-four hours a day, but most of the offices were darkened now after eight or nine o'clock.

Nevertheless, Tim felt an uneasy urge to return to the factory, to walk through the busy workrooms.

Everything seemed to be in order as he went from building to building. Wherever he looked he saw nothing but hard, conscientious work; busy men who fully realized the responsibility that was upon their shoulders. Yet, somewhere in that plant, he was beginning to feel, saboteurs were at work.

Myron Sumner, an experienced factory executive, had been installed as manager of this plant when the government took it over. With him from Washington had come Herbert Carrol, who was a trained aeronautical engineer; Ito Mabuchi, in his capacity as technical adviser; and Tim, who was anxious to have some part, however small, in speeding the production of these great ships on which so much depended.

Mabuchi had proved invaluable from the start. With his assistance, plans for the super-ships were soon drafted, construction crews swung smoothly into the work, and the great metal skeletons had begun to take shape almost over-night. Four of the ships were to be built at the same time—each sufficiently powerful to engage and annihilate Kasuga-Tosa's whole squadron, single-handed.

"Once these babies take to the air there will be an end to Kasuga!" Sumner had chuckled, as he made his daily inspection of the plant. "Another week and we'll be ready to give him the surprise of his life!"

But that night a terrific explosion demolished one of the factories, completely destroying the ship nearing completion.

Sumner had raged like a madman when he received the news. For two days he had devoted himself tirelessly in an investigation to place the responsibility for the disaster—but without result.

And that night two of the factories had caught fire.

Sumner was out of bed with the first alarm. A water-soaked, smoke-blackened scarecrow, he fought the flames beside his men, took chances from which they flinched, seemed to be all

124

over at once. Largely due to his efforts one of the buildings was saved and its precious content salvaged. But the other, with the half-built ship it sheltered, was a complete loss.

Those "accidents" had been too opportunely timed to be accepted as unavoidable mishaps. They were deliberate sabotage. Tim knew that. Myron Sumner knew it—and every man in the great aero-works knew it. Someone was skulking here among them, waiting for a chance to destroy all they had accomplished; someone who already had caused the death of nearly fifty of their fellow-workers.

That had a bad effect. It slowed up the excellent progress, and it drove Myron Sumner nearly frantic. After that, it seemed that he hardly slept. He was in the plant day and night, watching for trouble, driving the work onward, making of himself an example of tireless energy and devotion to his task.

But despite his watchfulness, things continued to go wrong. Little things, not major catastrophes like the first two. Yet small things that delayed the work and gradually dropped it behind schedule. Shipments of materials that could not be used, the manufacture of parts that would not fit when completed, the disappearance of vital parts that had to be remanufactured while the work was held up waiting for them. Little things—but indubitably a part of the program of time-wasting sabotage. Each contributed its bit to delay the completion of those ships; each added to America's great danger.

In spite of those delays, the rocket-ships were almost completed on this night when Tim Donovan returned uneasily

125

to the plant. Two days more, Mabuchi had said, and the ships would be ready for the air!

Now Sumner was taking added precautions. The guards had been doubled at every door, and even the block-distant approaches to the plant were being patrolled. Yet Tim was not wholly satisfied. No matter how he tried to talk himself out of his restlessness, he could not down the premonition of disaster that now hung over him.

A THOUSAND times Tim had asked himself who the guilty party could be. Someone right here in the plant, not someone from the outside—of that he was convinced. Someone who had the run of the plant and could move about without exciting suspicion. That seemed the logical answer.

But who?

Mabuchi? The Japanese was a logical suspect, but Tim had to admit that his conduct had been exemplary. He had worked as hard as anyone in speeding the construction—and even harder in striving to remedy the damage and make up for the delay these interruptions had caused.

Sumner? That seemed equally absurd—for Myron Sumner actually was losing weight, was becoming drawn and haggard, through his tireless slaving and constant worrying.

Herbert Carrol? Tim did not come in contact with Carrol as frequently as with the others. But the bitter hatred for the invaders, that now motivated the man's life, left little room for doubting him. Herbert Carrol would have been a married man now, had it not been for Kasuga-Tosa. Bea Halliday had prom-ised to become his bride the day after her opening in "Tomorrow

126

and Forever." But that "tomorrow" had never come, and now he faced a "forever" of regret and of bitter hatred.

Tim had caught a glimpse of the mad light that at times glowed in Carrol's eyes—a gleam that startled him and made him thankful that he had not incurred Herbert Carrol's enmity. Carrol the guilty man? Tim snorted. God help the saboteur if Herb Carrol laid hands on him!

Beyond those three men, the traitor might be anyone of thousands of workmen, foremen, superintendents, guards, clerks—a hopeless task to try to put a finger on him by process of elimination. And yet he was here, somewhere in the plant; more dangerous than ever now that the rocket-ships were so near to completion....

Everything seemed to be running smoothly in the great building-sheds, but Tim's uneasiness persisted. For no accountable reason his footsteps turned toward the offices. They were dark, as he expected; lit only by a night-light. At the outer doorway he hesitated, started to turn away, when he suddenly paused—almost certain that he had heard a slight, metallic-squeaking noise.

That was strange. It sounded like the door of the safe—and that had been closed before he left the office, not to be opened again until the next morning.

Carefully Tim stepped inside, passed through the small reception office and into the big room beyond, opening the connecting door with the greatest of care. And then he tensed.

Yes—the safe was open. A man was kneeling in front of it—was opening drawer after drawer, riffling his fingers through their contents. Tim edged nearer, close enough so that he could see the figure plainly while still keeping behind cover. That figure was familiar. Tim felt a little chill trickle down his spine—and then he was certain. The dim night-light that hung over the safe fell full—on the tense, tight-lipped face of Herbert Carrol.

Herb Carrol there, robbing the safe!

Tim heard him curse softly, saw him start to rise to his feet—and then he sprang bolt upright when the office lights snapped on, brilliantly. There, revolver in hand, his face set sternly, his eyes as grim as death, was Myron Sumner, striding forward like an executioner.

"Don't move, Carrol—or I'll let you have it!" he snapped. "I thought something like this would be the next move. We have the plant too carefully guarded for you, eh? So now you think you will cripple us this way. But you forgot that the front of this safe can be seen from the side window of the draughting room—where I happened to be."

Now he had reached the open safe door. Still holding the gun trained on Carrol, he stooped and pulled open one of the drawers—and then gasped in amazement that was edged with rage.

"By God, you *did* manage it!" he swore bitterly. "*Where are those plans,* Carrol? Put them back in that drawer!"

For a moment Tim thought that his finger must constrict too tightly on the trigger; thought that Carrol's doom was certain. But that white knuckle held death back by no more than a hair.

"That is what I want to know—where the plans are," Carrol said brittlely. "That is why I am here tonight—to satisfy myself that they are no longer in that safe there."

"You lie!" Sumner flung at him. "The plans were in that safe at eight o'clock when it was locked. Now it is open—*you* opened it—and now they are gone. I am not going to search you. You are too smart for that—but, wherever you have hidden them, you are not going to be able to reach them. I'm going to have you put under lock and key and kept there until I get in touch with Operator 5 and hear what he wants done with you."

And then Tim Donovan almost fell through the floor.

"All right, Tim; come out of there," Sumner called to him. "It's okay—don't worry. I know you had nothing to do with this. I saw you come in and watch him. Good thing you did—otherwise he probably would deny that he had even been in here."

Rather sheepishly Tim came out from behind the filing cabinet that had been his shelter. Obediently he followed Sumner to a little, windowless storeroom where he locked Carrol and then slipped the key into his pocket.

"I am going downstairs to get the police to jail him overnight, until I can contact Operator 5," he turned to Tim. "He will be all right in there—but maybe you had better stay outside here. Hang on to this—" he thrust the revolver into Tim's hand—"not that you will need it… but just to play safe."

Then he was gone….

WHEN SUMNER returned, five minutes later, Tim was just picking himself up from the floor; was clasping his hands to his skull, where an egg-sized bump was sending smarting pains through his head. The revolver was gone, and the door of the storeroom was open—its interior empty.

"Where is he? Where is Carrol?" Sumner demanded, shaking Tim's shoulder and shouting as if to batter a way through the lad's daze.

"I was sitting back there, watching the door," Tim mumbled. "I saw smoke coming out from under it—thought he had set the room on fire. I came over to the door to try to see under it—and then it flew open and I went down. That—that seems to be all I remember."

And Herbert Carrol made good his escape. The police searched the city for him the next day, but he was not found....

Myron Sumner received the news glumly.

"Fortunately, the loss of the plans no longer matter," he conceded. "The work on the ships is almost completed. Tomorrow they will be ready for their test flight—but until then I am not leaving this plant."

Restlessly he paced the factories that day, appearing and reappearing like a wraith, watching constantly. But it was Tim who saw the first sign of disaster and shouted the alarm. As he was going through one of the building-sheds, his eyes turned to the great air-monster so nearly ready to soar up into the heavens. Suddenly Tim tensed. There was a wisp of smoke, barely visible, coming out of one of the open ports!

Tim raced up one of the runways into the ship, and immediately he caught the smell of smoke, of burning oil! The ship was on fire! Breathlessly he dashed back down the runway and out of the shed to the cord of the emergency whistle. He tugged down hard, and the shrill warning blast keened out over the plant—to be blotted out by the all-engulfing roar of a terrific explosion.

Another and another.... Three in quick succession—and then three more.

The concussion knocked Tim to the ground, held him there while the heavens seemed to rain thudding, clattering debris—and when he picked himself up and looked dazedly around him the whole world seemed to be changed and unfamiliar. The great building-sheds were gone! Their roofs blown off by the thunderous explosions, their walls had collapsed—and tumbled in on the shattered, tangled wreckage of what had been America's unlaunched super-rocket-ships!

Tears streamed down Tim Donovan's face as he stared at that smoldering mass of junk that was all that remained of weeks of ceaseless labor, all that remained of the high hopes that had been so near to realization. The last ray of hope seemed to fade into nothing in that dismal moment. Tim hardly heard Myron Sumner raving beside him; hardly heard the man moaning that it would take weeks to rebuild those buildings, more weeks to build new ships—*even if they had had the plans.*

Tim knew all that, and he knew that the plans were gone. Bitterly he stared down at the blast-torn wreckage. In it he saw the end of America's dream of liberty....

Sumner was a raging madman after he had recovered from his initial shock. Immediately he launched an investigation that he swore would not be dropped until he had his fingers on the throat of the man responsible for that destruction. But Tim did not wait to learn its results.

Two facts he did learn, and they were sufficient.

One was that Ito Mabuchi had disappeared. Whether or not

he had been blown to atoms by the blasts that chewed up the rocket-ships as if they were made of paper, no man knew—but he was gone. The other discovery was that Myron Sumner's apartment had been burglarized shortly before the explosion, his safe blown open and his belongings thoroughly ransacked—by a man whose description, furnished by the building superintendent, corresponded with that of Herbert Carrol.

Tim waited for no more. With a heavy heart he headed for Fort Ticonderoga—to greet Operator 5 in his moment of triumph with the news that victory had been snatched from his grasp by treachery!

Now there was no longer a reason for struggling to hold the invaders back from Schenectady. Now there was no alternative but to tell the elated defenders that their splendid effort had been in vain—that there was nothing left but to retreat....

CHAPTER 9
DESTRUCTION'S PATH

WITH THE abandonment of Ticonderoga, the great blot of devastation now spread to the west and south. Albany and Schenectady went up in flames, and the invaders swept the Hudson Valley with a bath of fire. Closer and closer to New York City the scourge crept, while Operator 5 made desperate preparations to defend the metropolis.

More than half of New York's population had fled by this time, but thousands answered his call for volunteers and hurried to the armories to await orders. There the skeleton organization, which he had hastily assembled, was already at work, interviewing and testing the applicants, dividing them into two classes—those who would make a last, desperate stand against the invaders north of the city, and those who would remain behind, until the last hope was gone.

It was to these latter that Jimmy addressed himself.

"I don't want thrill-seekers or would-be heroes who expect to cover themselves with glory—I want martyrs!" he told them bluntly. "I want men willing to resign themselves to death when they undertake this task—men willing to die in the attempt to trap these invaders.

"Almost certain death is what you will face—not merely the hazards of the battlefield," he warned solemnly. "I want men who are willing to stay behind after the city is abandoned. They will man guns to be concealed in the upper floors of our tallest buildings; others must go down under the streets into the steam tunnels, carrying loads of explosives. They will set these off beneath the invaders' ships. I need volunteers who are willing to face the great-headed men and bait them into dynamite traps. That is what we must face. I will be there with you."

A few there were who quailed at that prospect.

Jimmy spotted them quickly and dismissed them. But his assistants had done their work well. Nearly every one of those volunteers grunted a quick acceptance or merely nodded their heads in grim acquiescence.

Six hundred of them Jimmy chose—a modern Light Brigade whose deeds were to dwarf into insignificance the performance of their balladed predecessors. Six hundred men who were to walk into the jaws of death not because someone had blundered but with their eyes *open*—because this could be the one hope for the country which they loved more than life itself....

Twentieth Century Minute Men, those volunteers went back to their homes to wait for the signal that would call them to doom. Theirs was now the task of waiting, but for Jimmy Christopher and his immediate aides endless details remained to be arranged, wearisome preparations to be made. Big guns must be smuggled into the city at night and taken to the highest floors of Manhattan's skyscrapers, loads of high explosives to be stored where they would be readily accessible, watchers to be posted, a system of alarms to be arranged. Endless details—while the huge black scar, that marked the trail of Kasuga-Tosa on the map, drew ever closer.

Yonkers went up in flames; White Plains, Mount Vernon, New Rochelle—while the twenty percent of New York's population that still clung to the city trembled in apprehension. Desperately the ragged army, that was attempting to bar the way, strove to thrust the invaders back. But that downward sweep was irresistible. Finally the last lines of the defenders broke—they were scattered, blasted like leaves before the rush of a forest fire.

New York's moment had come!

Great beacons penciled the night from the tip of the Statue of Liberty's torch; alternating red and white, the warning to flee—that the invaders were at the door and liberty was no more. Instantly the panicky exodus began; by cars, by boats, by tubes and bridges—any way to escape the doom that hung over Manhattan Island.

The sirens that sped those fleeing thousands on their way also assembled the volunteers who were to stay behind. To half a dozen central points the volunteers hurried, and there Jimmy's assistants detailed them to their posts—patriots rushing through the empty streets of a deserted city to keep a rendezvous with death!

OPERATOR 5 had slept almost beside his desk in those tense days. The moment the warning sounded, he was up from the cot, where he had been snatching a brief nap—and was at his telephone. The line was still open, manned by one of his own men, now that the panic-stricken operators had fled. And over it came flashes that quickly indicated the extent of the disaster.

The last semblance of resistance from the defending army had been shattered, and the great-headed men were streaming down into the Bronx, backed by one of their rocket-ships now spreading flames on every side. But that was not all. Simultaneously, the other two ships had launched an attack on the city.

"One of them came down in Foley Square," the excited voice of the undercover man reported. "They are pouring downtown, setting the whole lower part of the city on fire. The gunners in the Woolworth Building have just opened up—but the whole building is ablaze, and those little bullet-ships are buzzing around it like hornets. The other ship is down in Park Avenue, just above Forty-fifth Street. Everything was ablaze up there when the last line from that exchange went dead."

Now the telephone was practically useless, but Jimmy had foreseen that emergency. Couriers were already starting to arrive at the midtown hotel in which he had established his headquarters. And they brought reports of nothing but tragedy.

The invaders were irresistible, sweeping everything before them, turning the whole island into a flaming holocaust. The volunteers were sticking to their posts, were dying there as the flames engulfed them—but failing... failing utterly.

Now Jimmy could wait no longer. It was time for his last effort, the ace he had been holding up his sleeve.

Twenty-three of the pick of his own men and the volunteers were waiting for him in the outer office. They rose to their feet the moment he appeared in the doorway. Downstairs automobiles were waiting for them at the front of the hotel. These sped them to a garage where they got out and waited while Jimmy pressed a lever that parted the rear wall in the middle and drew the sides apart as if they had been curtains.

In the big room beyond that wall were six low-built armored cars that looked like miniature tanks. Tanks that were armed with high-power field pieces and battering-ram prows that came to a knife-sharp edge and point. Those cars were sheathed with the new flame-proof steel—sides, tops and even bottoms. Six miniature juggernauts that would hurl themselves at the huge rocket-ships.

Four men to a car, they took their places, and the strange-looking fleet sped across town to Park Avenue.

Jimmy Christopher's eyes narrowed grimly when he beheld that once fashionable residential street. Now it was a canyon of flames, a raging inferno—and there in the middle of the pavement was the huge monster that had loosed destruction upon it. From Jimmy's car a deep whistle sounded, once—and the squadron rounded a corner and headed for its objective.

A wave of gas met them. Toward them came charging nearly fifty of the big-headed men, their projectors leveled and operating—but there was no resulting spark and flash of flames. The armor-plate had stood the test! The cars were hurtling forward, now less than a block from the rocket-ship—when suddenly the whole street was flushed with a dark liquid that spread over it like a wave flattening out on a sandy beach. A wave that came from the invaders' craft....

Oil! Too late Jimmy realized what it was! In the same split-second it burst into roaring flame!

Three of the cars were completely engulfed by the sudden blaze. The others were into it before they could apply their brakes. Of the six, the one in which Jimmy rode was the last to be engulfed. Desperately the driver jammed on his brakes and bent over the wheel, turning, trying frantically to swerve the car in that skiddy surface.

The flames were all around them, licking at the windows, turning the car into a virtual oven. They would be baked alive, would roast there in the flames—but the other cars were already in that raging hell, and Jimmy would not turn back. Leaning over the driver, he clutched the wheel, attempted to turn it, to whip the car back onto its course straight into the rocket-ship.

But his men stopped him. Two of them seized him and pulled him clear; dragged him back into the car and held them there. "No, Operator 5—it's no use!" one of them panted. "We will be roasted alive—for no use!"

He struggled furiously, but they clung to him and would not release their hold until at last the driver managed to steer the smoking, sizzling hot car out of that inferno and into a side street. Of the six cars that had made that charge, theirs was the sole survivor—the only one to be snatched from the flaming jaws of hell. Jimmy's struggles subsided when he realized that his men had saved him from what would have been a horrible and useless suicide. The rocket-ships seemed to be invulnerable, and New York City was at their mercy. In a few hours Manhattan Island would be a raging bonfire from tip to tip.

ON THE west bank of the Hudson, Operator 5 and his surviving aides did their best to rally the routed troops. Restoring them to at least a semblance of order, he led the way south, through New Jersey and into Pennsylvania. And hot on their heels came the invaders.

Jersey City, Trenton and Reading were reduced to ashes—and Philadelphia lay directly in the path of the flames. Hopelessly Jimmy tried to put up a defense, but the result was a foregone conclusion. His men were routed, driven headlong into the almost deserted city.

Without resistance the invaders swept through the suburbs and into the heart of the city in advance of their rocket-ships. Steadily the flames ate their way forward, until the destroyers swarmed into Independence Square and the cradle of American liberty lay before them. Billowing gas bathed it, and the ray-projectors turned upon it—but, amazingly, Independence Hall resisted the flames!

Instantly the hovering rocket-ship took note of that amazing phenomenon and saw the blistering machine-gun fire that poured from the old building. Quickly a hundred of their great-headed slaves were rushed up to the hall, to batter in the door and smash their way inside, while the air-monster hung above the roof, curious but suspicious.

And then it seemed that the whole square blew up!

The belfry was torn apart with a terrific crash, the wrecking fingers of the high-explosive charge reaching in vain for the mammoth hell-ship just overhead. A daring trap—but it had failed!

Echoing that thunderous crash came others—nearly a dozen of them—and before the last had hurled its tons of debris heavenward Independence Hall was no more.

It had vanished with most of the square—and with it had gone Professor Seymour Durant and his son, the secret of the flame-resisting preparation, with which they had painted the building, forever lost with them.

The smoking, dismally settling heap of wreckage that was all that remained of America's shrine of liberty became a tomb and a monument for them and for twenty others who had thought themselves pacifists—yet, in their deaths, had proved themselves American heroes....

WHILE JIMMY CHRISTOPHER was struggling to stem the destructive tide, those whom he had left behind had not been idle. His Washington office was a place of constant activity as old John Christopher worked tirelessly to establish a corps of modern Paul Reveres who would spread the word of the on-coming destroyers by swiftly racing motorcycles from

With a wild yell, the Americans broke from their hiding-places!

INVASION FROM THE SKY

town to town; to organize a brigade of volunteers who would remain in each abandoned town to meet the invaders and fight them to the death.

His blood pounded in his veins as he enlisted those young martyrs. The call to join them and face their doom was strong within him—but his weakened body forbade any such attempt. Q-6 sighed; at least he could serve in this capacity while Operator 5 was in the field.

Another who had been working night and day was Norman King. Proceeding on a plan sketched by Jimmy, he and his staff were striving to perfect a defense against the rocket-ships. Every effort against them had been a complete failure. It seemed that they could not be stopped—and yet at last he and his assistants hit upon a trap that must work.

That trap required a great deal of equipment, but American industry answered with a will. Factories had worked night and day—and by the time Operator 5 returned to the partly wrecked capital, in advance of the straggling mob that had once been an army, the weapon for which he had been longing was now ready at hand.

Camden had fallen after Philadelphia. Wilmington was the next to go up in flames, and Baltimore appeared doomed that gloomy evening when a battered army car delivered him outside Norman King's laboratory. America seemed lost, doomed, at that moment—but King's first words brought new hope surging up within him.

"The balloons are here, Operator 5!" he greeted triumphantly. "Four carloads of them arrived this afternoon, and we already have three carloads of cable—all silicate-amalgamed. We can start putting the protection around Washington in the morning."

"Not Washington—Baltimore," Jimmy overruled quickly. "And not in the morning, Doc. We're starting tonight—right away!"

Within half an hour a long string of army trucks was filing up to those seven freight cars and then heading for the highway to Baltimore. There Jimmy Christopher waited to receive them with a throng of eager mechanics. All through the night they worked unloading the trucks and converting their contents into a great barricade that would bar the way from the north.

That barricade was invisible when they had finished. Behind buildings and clumps of trees, at regularly spaced intervals, lay great deflated balloons—with the mechanism that would inflate them already attached to their nozzles. Balloons that had mighty lifting power and were made of a material that would defy the fire-gas of the invaders. These balloons were attached to a thick cable, miles long—a cable which, when raised, would suspend below it a web of cables to a depth of half a mile.

By dawn that army of willing workmen had the balloons moored, the net stretched and everything covered so that it would be invisible to all save those who knew exactly where to look for it. Invisible—yet ready to shoot skyward a few minutes after the waiting Signal Corps men received word that the rocket-ships were on their way.

Behind the wire-cable snare Jimmy massed his defenders—the remnants of the fleeing troops from Philadelphia and the embattled citizens of Baltimore, who were grimly determined to be in at the death of this aerial destroyer that threatened to wipe out their city. Eager man-power—and, backing them up, cleverly concealed batteries of artillery that would be turned loose the moment it was in the trap.

Jimmy sighed with profound relief when that task was finished and he could telephone to Alexandria and tell Andrew Warren that the trap was set. They would not have long to wait for Kasuga-Tosa, of that he was certain—but before the rocket-ships appeared another visitor arrived who brought a worried frown to Jimmy's face.

It was President Warren.

"If they are ready to risk their lives so gallantly, who am I to stay hiding at home?" he protested with a tired smile when Jimmy took him to task for coming into the danger zone.

With the President had come General Logan, the chief-of-staff, and several of his subordinates, among whom Myron Sumner was now listed.

Andrew Warren never would comprehend the importance of his life to America, Jimmy thought, as the visitors were making their inspection—and even as that thought flashed through his mind his fears were realized. From the building where he had been on duty one of the Signal Corps men now came running excitedly.

"They are on the way!" he shouted. "Havre de Grace is burning, and two of the ships have already been started this way!"

Vainly Jimmy tried to induce Warren to go back to Washington or Alexandria.

The President was adamant.

"They are not running away, and neither shall I," he said firmly. "Don't worry, Jimmy—I shall not be in your way. I'll remain back here at headquarters with General Logan without any—"

The wail of the warning sirens cut him short. Jimmy dashed out and hurried toward the waiting trap. Now he would have to gamble. The ships were reported coming on fast, less than twenty miles away—a matter of only a few minutes. If the trap was sprung too late it would be useless; if too early, the Japanese might see it and veer away.

A matter of minutes, seconds, one way or the other.... Jimmy gauged the exact time as well as he could and then gave the order to fill the balloons and let go.

UP INTO the air they went—just as the rocket-ships appeared, no more than specks in the distance. Jimmy held his breath; he knew the incredible speed of those monsters. And then he groaned. One of the enemy ships was past the snare, was overhead, gliding down now into the city. But the other arrived a few seconds too late! It ran squarely into the suspended cables, whipped the balloons down halfway to the ground and threatened to carry away the whole web. But the cables held. The rocket-ship settled to the ground. Before it could belch forth its dangerous gas, the hidden batteries poured salvos of shells into it. With a wild yell, the waiting American defenders broke from their hiding-places, ignoring Jimmy's warning to wait until he gave the word for a charge. Their enthusiasm had been too much for them. Vainly Jimmy shouted a warning, tried to sound the recall, as he took after them. Before he was halfway to the ship the disaster he feared overwhelmed them. Suddenly, like a giant squid, the leviathan erupted great clouds of thick, inky-black smoke that settled to the ground and extended for blocks in almost every direction.

In that Stygian fog his men were helpless. Jimmy caught a glimpse of the doors of the giant craft opening, the monstrous-headed creatures flocking out—and then the black wave engulfed him. All around him he heard the groans and death-screams of men who were being cut down mercilessly—victims who did not even see the direction from which death scythed them down.

Blindly he turned and started to grope his way forward, vainly seeking light—some way out of this sea of darkness.... Men crashed into him and almost knocked him down. Bodies under-foot tripped him and almost tumbled him headlong. Then one of those metal-helmeted figures loomed in front of him. Instantly Myron Sumner materialized out of the gloom and flung himself at the creature.

They struggled desperately, but before Jimmy could leap to Sumner's assistance the darkness had swallowed them up. Out of that darkness came a blow that crashed down on Jimmy's head.

He went down... and then someone was standing over him, picking him up, carrying him—Myron Sumner. That was the last thing Jimmy knew before the blackness blotted out every-thing completely....

WHEN HE returned to consciousness he was in a cellar; a safe hiding-place to which his men had carried him, he found.

Now the ship was gone and the blanket of inky fog was lifting, evaporating. Gradually he remembered those last few moments before he went down—remembered Myron Sumner.

"Sumner? He's all right," one of the men answered his question. "We found him lying out there on the street near you. He was knocked out, but he came around all right when we got him out of the smoke."

Already much of Baltimore was in ruins. Operator 5 saw that the moment he got to his feet and walked uncertainly to the cellar door.

But where was Andrew Warren? That question brought a chill to Jimmy's heart, for nobody in that cellar could answer it. He *must* know. With three of the men who volunteered to go with him, he stepped out into the precarious street. Blazing buildings were crumbling everywhere, showering the sidewalk with wreckage. Cautiously, he made his way back toward his headquarters.

Like the rest of the block in which it stood, the flaming building appeared deserted. But in the big front room of the lower floor he stumbled over the blistered body of Daniel Logan. Although dying, the general was still conscious.

"The President—where is he?" Jimmy said in his ear.

Back came the answer he dreaded. "They've got him," Logan croaked. "I tried to save him—but they cut me down. One of those devils in a helmet—shorter than the rest—recognized Warren. They carried him away."

Swiftly his mind began to cast about for a way to combat that disastrous reaction. He must get to Alexandria at once, before the reports of President Warren's capture could be veri-fied—before Vice-President Clarman Tobey had a chance to take any action.

Jimmy had little confidence in Tobey. The man was a poseur, a politician and not a statesman. His dignified appearance was imposing, but Jimmy suspected that it was little more than "front." No character or courage was behind it.

Those troublesome thoughts rode with him all the way, as he drove at reckless speed to Alexandria. When he stepped into the mansion that was Tobey's temporary office and residence he saw at once that his worst fears were to be realized. Tobey had heard of Andrew Warren's disappearance—and already he was beginning to go to pieces under the responsibility that had suddenly descended upon him.

"I warned him that he was wrong in his headstrong oppo-sition to the inevitable," Tobey rushed his words and avoided Jimmy's disconcerting stare. "We cannot oppose these invaders. Their weapons are invincible. To continue to oppose them will mean only a steadily increasing loss of life—and defeat in the end. If Andrew Warren had listened to me, our great Eastern cities would be standing today—and he would still be safe in Washington.

"I intend to make peace with Kasuga-Tosa," Tobey said doggedly. "I am going to radio an invitation to him to meet me—"

The words withered and died on his lips; lips that suddenly were drained of all color as his eyes widened until they threat-ened to pop out of his head. Those eyes were staring into the black muzzle of an automatic that was now trained on his quaking belly.

"No, you aren't, Tobey," Jimmy's voice was hard and icy cold. "You are not going to betray America—not while I am alive to stop you. You are coming with me—to a place where you will have no opportunity to be stampeded by your own cowardice."

And in that moment Operator 5, the man to whom the very idea of a dictatorship was abhorrent, decided that, to save America, he would take command of the nation....

CHAPTER 10
DOUBLE TRAP

THE UNITED STATES was not left in doubt very long about the fate of its President. Kasuga-Tosa promptly released two of his women captives, who came running with the story of Warren's capture. After that, the tactics of the invader changed. Dropping his pose of unmotivated scourge, he boldly revealed himself in his true colors. Over Washington and a dozen other cities his rocket-ships scattered leaflets bearing his proclamation to the nation.

"Surrender unconditionally and immediately, or face merciless extermination," was the essence of that message—and to give it weight his raiders lashed out with savagery even more vicious than before.

A score of little towns and villages in Maryland and Pennsylvania were wiped off the map in that beastly demonstration—and the tales of atrocious barbarity that came from the lips of the horrified survivors made Jimmy Christopher's blood run cold. There was no indecision, no question in his own mind about the course on which he was embarked. But now he could not escape the haunting feeling that everyone of those ghastly deaths was on his own head.

To stop it there could be only one course of action.

From the radio stations of the nation now was broadcast an answer of defiance, over the signature of Clarman Tobey—and the listeners who heard it coming through their loudspeakers little realized the conditions under which it was signed. Those bold words gave no hint of the cringing captive who cowered at the very sight of Jimmy Christopher's unholstered gun—and then, his signature scrawled to the statement, took out his sorry spite in taunting, venomous threats.

"That is the signature to the death warrant of countless thousands of men and women," Tobey had snarled, as the pen dropped from his fingers. "But it is not my signature, Operator 5—it is yours. You are murdering those people, not I—and I will see to it that you are held personally responsible for every life that is needlessly sacrificed!"

A threat that Jimmy knew the man would be only too happy to be able to carry out—and, if Andrew Warren was killed by his captors, Clarman Tobey *would* be president of the United States. Jimmy was well aware of that possibility—and the knowledge made him realize that he stood entirely alone. If he succeeded in driving out the invaders, Henry Tobey's hatred would be of no importance—but if he failed, then Tobey would have his day. A day that would mean disgrace and possibly even death for the discredited Operator 5....

SPURNING THE half-wrecked national capital, Kasuga-Tosa had swung northwestward, over Pennsylvania and into New York. Reading, Harrisburg, Wilkes-Barre, Scranton—city after city became a smoking ruin as the vandals passed. And now he mocked at the efforts to spread a warning in advance of his coming; contemptuously scorned the attempts to oppose him.

Arrogantly he announced *in advance* the cities that would be next destroyed!

With haggard, tired eyes Jimmy studied the map spread out before him; stared at the constantly spreading blot of destruction that was enveloping the entire northeast corner of the United States. New England was in ruins, New York was wiped clean of its principal cities—stripped of all but Rochester and Buffalo. Rochester was beyond saving; the invaders were sweeping down upon it that very day. Buffalo would be next.

But here Kasuga-Tosa must be checked! Beyond the great lakeport he must not be allowed to go—or there would be no stopping him until the flames he kindled were lapping at the very shores of the Pacific!

Somehow, those rocket-ships must be stopped, destroyed—but how? Jimmy had faced that question so many times that it had become a perpetual nightmare to haunt him night and day. There *must* be an answer to it, and there was—a fighting chance....

It was Norman King who furnished it, although there was

little trace of his usual enthusiasm in his voice when he telephoned from Washington.

"We are on the trail of something big—something that can be of vital importance, Operator 5," he reported. "But it persists in eluding us—distractingly. We have perfected a ray-projector that will overcome the rocket-ships' combustion and stall them—but the trouble is that we can't seem to develop sufficient power to carry over any appreciable distance. At a few hundred yards, fine—but farther than that our projector will *not* reach. If we could only develop sufficient power to reach up and drag them down from the sky—"

A projector that would stall the rocket-ships once they were within its radius, once they were on the ground…. Jimmy's thoughts were shuttling at top speed, planning, envisioning possibilities…. His blood tingled, and a great hope began to dawn within him!

"How many of those projectors are you using for your experiments, Doc?" he demanded eagerly.

"We have six here in the laboratory—but we also have sufficient parts to rig up twice as many more if they will be of any use to you," King answered doubtfully.

"Get busy on them, Doc!" Jimmy's voice was elated. "Send me those you have, by plane immediately—and the others as soon as they are completed. We have the answer at last! Now we can fight!"

Quickly he called his staff together and outlined the plan that was already full-blown in his mind.

"We will let him take Buffalo, gentlemen, but only after what must appear to be a desperate defense," he announced. "When the rocket-ships come down to complete their destruction, they will be in our hands. We can tell pretty well where they will alight—in front of the Grand Union Station, probably. We will be prepared for them there—and also at the other most likely landing points.

"In the buildings around those points we will have out ray-projectors waiting. They will go into action as soon as the ships are down—will cripple and hold them there, helpless to escape. Beneath those squares we must concentrate every ounce of high explosive that we can lay our hands upon. Most of Buffalo must be blown off the face of the earth, gentlemen— but the rocket-ships will go with them! Once we have them grounded, they will be at the mercy of the mines beneath them!

"That will take men who are not afraid to face certain death," his voice became grave. "We have enlisted martyr battalions before—but those had at least a *chance* of escape. These men will have none. I need at least five hundred volunteers to stay in Buffalo after it is evacuated and will fight to the death; men who will stay there and be blown into eternity when the city is destroyed. That is the only way we can be sure of baiting Kasuga-Tosa into our trap."

Swiftly they went to work. The army engineers cleared whole square blocks of the city, while their sappers mined under the pavement from the cellars of the buildings. As soon as those excavations were ready, they were packed tight with explosives that were wired to central switches. At the same time an army of mechanics sheathed the fronts of the buildings, facing those

DIANE

ANDREW WARREN

DR. NORMAN KING

MAUREEN DURANT

155

squares with fireproof armor-plate. The moment the projectors arrived from Washington they were set up in carefully selected positions—and the preparations were completed except for the men who must play such a vital part in the trap's springing.

There was no difficulty enlisting that battalion; the problem was to hold down in size to the required number.

Everything was in readiness... but at the eleventh hour disaster loomed from a totally unexpected source! It was a telephone call from John Christopher, in Washington, that apprised Operator 5 of the danger.

"Congress is weakening, Jimmy," he warned. "The peace-at-any-price element is winning new converts. That ultimatum of Kasuga-Tosa's was just what they needed to swing a lot of wavering votes their way. They have recessed for today, but I'm afraid that both houses will be stampeded in the morning and then surrender before noon."

Surrender now, when victory was almost within his grasp! That dismaying prospect stunned Jimmy... but only for a moment. Then he began to seek the plan that would ward off this disaster. He would have to go to Washington at once, buttonhole the Congressional leaders and convince them of their mistake. If necessary, he must bargain with them to win at least a twenty-four hour respite.

Then, if he failed and Buffalo was destroyed in vain, he would no longer be able to hold in check the peace-at-any-price movement.

OPERATOR 5'S field headquarters, on the edge of Batavia, was almost deserted on the evening Maureen Durant reached it.

156

Returning, discouraged and down-hearted, after nearly a week of unsuccessful attempts to contact the girls in Kasuga-Tosa's rocket-ships, they found that Jimmy was gone and most of his aides were in Buffalo, preparing for that city's defense. Outside Batavia were the American entrenchments, manned by the weary troops who had been driven back helplessly from town to town.

This defense would be hopeless, too, Diane admitted to herself in a surge of pessimism; everything was hopeless. There was nobody in the field headquarters who was able to deny the logic of that despondent outlook. Colonel Walters was up in the lines, endeavoring to strengthen the morale of his men, and the young officers in his tent knew nothing of the trap Operator 5 planned. Deliberately that information had been held from them for fear they might unconsciously betray it to the men, who, in turn, would allow the knowledge to effect their resistance.

This trap *must* work. Jimmy had taken no chances that any little slip might arouse the suspicion of the enemy and hold the rocket-ships off, out of reach of the waiting projectors. Only the major officers and the engineers knew the details of those plans.

Where had Operator 5 gone?

The young officers were not certain about that either. He had left late in the afternoon in a plane; and one of them thought he had heard the pilot instructed to set a course for Washington—but the informant could not be sure about that.

Disappointed and annoyed, Diane was about to return to

157

Batavia and seek a night's lodging for herself and Maureen, when a sergeant appeared in the doorway with a slip of paper.

"Two of our men just picked up this code message, sir," he reported to the captain in charge. "It came from the direction of Buffalo and seemed to have been sent by magnesium beacon. The code is unfamiliar—"

Magnesium beacon! Diane's interest was arrested immediately, and she was ready at the captain's side when he looked up, puzzled and surprised, from the unintelligible cipher. Many times, cut off from every other means of communication, she and Jimmy Christopher and Tim Donovan had used small magnesium beacons to flash messages to one another. When she glanced down at the sergeant's notation, she saw at once that the code was one that was known only to the three of them. That message was from Jimmy or Tim.

"Located in the Statler Hotel in Buffalo," she quickly decoded. "Following important lead but need feminine assistance immediately. Prefer Diane but other personable young woman will do. Speedy arrival is essential. Please do not fail." The message was from Jimmy. It had been worded for either her or for Tim Donovan, coded so that only they would be able to understand it. For some reason, it seemed, Jimmy did not want these officers to know where he was or what he was doing.

"For a moment the code looked familiar—but it isn't what I expected," she said coolly as she handed the slip back to the officer.

But Maureen Durant was not deceived.

"That message was from Operator 5," she accused. "You are

going to him—and I am going with you, Diane. You can't refuse me."

Jimmy's message said that he needed feminine assistance, Diane considered swiftly. Perhaps there would be an opportunity to utilize Maureen also.

"All right," she agreed, "you can come with me. We are going to Buffalo, as soon as I can get hold of a car."

"Buffalo—alone, you two girls—and at this time of night?" a reproving voice suddenly interrupted, and Myron Sumner stepped out of the darkness beside them.

"I couldn't help overhearing you just now," Sumner confessed. "You are going to Operator 5—but I know right well he would not allow you to tackle that trip alone. I know just where to locate him, in the Statler. If you insist on going tonight, you will have to tolerate a second-rate chauffeur."

AS THEY sped along Diane peered at the streets, at the briefly illuminated buildings. She was familiar with the layout of Buffalo, and it did not seem to her that Sumner was going in the right direction to reach the Statler. Unless she was badly confused by the darkness, the hotel was in quite another part of the city.

Now she was sure of it. This street was close to the lake, nowhere near the station—but before she could question him he brought the car to a stop in a pitch-dark alley at the side door of what appeared to be a large warehouse.

"This isn't the Statler," she protested, as he switched off the motor. "You said you knew the way."

"Of course, it's not," Sumner grinned. "We can't go directly to the hotel. We'll have to stop in here first, until I make sure that the way is clear. Can't take chances—"

The way clear in an *empty* city? That didn't make sense; didn't ring true. Suddenly Diane felt a wave of suspicion sweep over her. The little hairs at the back of her neck seemed to rise as she glanced at that ominous-looking building and then at Sumner holding the door open for them to get out. Suddenly she knew that she did not trust this man—realized that he had no intention of taking them to Jimmy!

Sumner sensed her suspicion at the same time—and when her fingers surreptitiously opened the catch of her handbag so that she could get at the automatic it contained, she found herself staring into a gun muzzle. Sumner was glaring at her with cold eyes that peered out of a face now terribly transformed.

"No, you don't!" he sneered, as he snatched the bag from her lap. "Get out, and make it snappy. Don't think I have any compunction about slapping this gun down over your head."

He meant that, she knew. His voice was brittle, steel-hard, and yet it quivered ever so slightly with excitement. Now he was watching her like a wolf, keeping the gun carefully trained on her as she stepped out onto the sidewalk. Maureen's handbag joined her own in his hand, and then he backed to the warehouse door, inserted a key in the lock and opened it.

Helplessly they stepped inside. His flashlight picked the way down a long corridor and to a rear room that was small and windowless, ventilated only by a grating-covered opening near the ceiling, Diane noted at once. He prodded them inside and motioned them to a rough bench that was the room's only furniture.

"So you have decided to show your true colors at last, have you?" Diane eyed him contemptuously, as she sank onto the bench. "May I ask what you intend to do with us now?"

"You certainly may—and I'll answer you, too," Sumner's voice throbbed with elation. "I am going to keep you here for a few hours, until my friend Ito Mabuchi arrives to pay you a visit."

"So that is the answer." Diane nodded her head understandingly. "A traitor who has sold out to the Japanese! That, of course, is also the answer to the series of accidents that destroyed the rocket-ships you were manufacturing. You and Mabuchi!"

"I see you know Mabuchi." He grinned crookedly as he saw the revulsion in her face. "Don't worry; you are not for him. You're worth too much to us for that. You are being reserved for Kasuga-Tosa. The old boy was smitten with you the first time he saw you and professes to be very anxious to renew your acquaintance.

"There is no accounting for tastes," he shrugged, "but I have a hunch that maybe it isn't altogether your charming personality that makes Kasuga so eager to get hold of you. Operator 5's sweetheart in his hands will give him a nice little weapon to hold over Jimmy Christopher's head—one that ought to bring Jimmy to terms and put an end to this silly resistance. But that's Kasuga-Tosa's business.

"Your Operator 5 happens to be in Washington," he chuckled. "Before he left, he was very busy making preparations to blow this city to pieces in order to trap Kasuga-Tosa when the

161

rocket-ships arrive tomorrow. But that clever little scheme isn't going to work. I shall have to leave you while I send a message back to headquarters. It will take care of that. When your friends know that you will be killed the moment the trap is sprung, I rather doubt that they will be so eager to start the fireworks."

For a moment he hesitated at the door; then it closed and utter blackness encompassed them. But that was infinitely preferable to the sight of Myron Sumner's shameless face.

Sitting there in the Stygian dark, Diane's dejected spirit plummeted to a new low. Word for word, she went over everything Sumner had said—and realized that his cunning scheme might indeed, succeed.

The Americans there in Buffalo, suspecting nothing of his duplicity, would accept him as a member of Operator 5's staff. They would unquestioningly take his message back to headquarters—a message that was certain to ruin all of Jimmy's plans if it had the effect Sumner anticipated.

If Jimmy was still away when that message arrived, his subordinates would not spring the trap; Diane was almost certain of that. They would not take the responsibility of condemning her to death. But if Jimmy had returned from Washington, then there was a chance….

"Please, God," her silent prayer went out through the darkness, "give him strength to go through with this if it will mean the salvation of America!"

CHAPTER 11
THE JAWS OF DEATH

THE TASK that confronted Operator 5 in Washington was even greater than he had feared. In fact the situation was so grave that he did not dare leave the capitol until he had made a personal appeal to the combined houses of Congress, prevailing upon them to take no action until after he had had a chance to spring his Buffalo *coup*. That left very little time, if he was to be back in Buffalo when the rocket-ships made their appearance.

Taking the controls of the army plane, himself, for the return trip, he coaxed every ounce of speed he could get from the racing motor. And as he sped northward his brain surged with a multitude of thoughts—not the least of which was a poignant regret for the probable fate of Andrew Warren.

A prisoner on one of the rocket-ships, it was extremely unlikely that the President would survive the trap, if the ships were destroyed—and yet there was nothing Jimmy could do to save him. Knowing Andrew Warren as he did, he was sure that the President would have sternly forbidden any thought of abandoning the *coup* so that his life might be spared.

When Jimmy's plane landed on the edge of Batavia, and he strode into the defense headquarters, a new and staggering angle of the problem confronted him. Gravely Colonel Walters looked up from his littered desk and handed him a sheet of paper.

"To Operator 5, or whoever may be in charge at the American defense headquarters," the heavily inked letters leaped out

163

at him. "This note will be delivered to you from Buffalo, where I am holding prisoner Miss Diane Elliot and Miss Maureen Durant. These ladies are being lodged in the center of town, directly over the mines which you intend to detonate on the arrival of Kasuga-Tosa's rocket-ships.

"Needless to point out, the setting off of these mines will seal their fate. But their lives will be spared and returned to you unharmed if you make peace with Kasuga-Tosa before the grace period expires. So far as I am concerned, rest assured that I shall be at a safe distance before the explosions occur. It is only the girls you will condemn to death by following out your present plans."

And the note bore the signature of Myron Sumner!

Myron Sumner, a traitor and a blackguard! Through Jimmy's mind kaleidoscoped a dozen little incidents that now stood out starkly revealed in a new light, and he groaned inwardly. He had been blind, utterly blind! And now his blindness had doomed Diane! For there was no other course than to go through with the plan; nothing to do but let the trap be sprung—allow the rending explosion to tear her lovely body into shreds. America must come first…. Through the mist that dimmed his eyes, Jimmy Christopher seemed to see Diane's sweet face smiling at him; he could almost hear her telling him that she understood, that it was all right. But what he actually heard was Colonel Walters' voice, calm and deliberate.

"The decision is now yours to make, Operator 5," he was saying. "If you had not arrived on time, I intended to cancel the orders and *not* spring the trap. Not only because of those young ladies, but because I think their deaths would be in vain. Now that we know that Myron Sumner has been in league with the enemy, it is only reasonable to suppose that he will find some way to communicate with Kasuga-Tosa and warn him. That will mean that the rocket-ships will avoid the trap."

Walters was right. This note of Sumner's was merely a piece of trickery, an attempt to induce the nation to surrender. If it failed, Kasuga-Tosa would no doubt be prepared for the trap that awaited him. He would blast the hidden projector-men from their concealment, *before* his ships came within range of their combustion-deadening rays.

"I should have seen that myself, Colonel," Jimmy admitted, as the truth of Walters' deductions came home to him. "You are right. We can't go through with it. The odds are all against us—too overwhelming to justify our sacrificing these lives, and probably that of the President as well. Please notify the men that their orders are canceled."

Jimmy Christopher felt years older, as he turned away from that desk.

Colonel Walters got busy on the telephone immediately, but in a few minutes his brow knotted perplexedly. Then gradually his face paled.

"It seems to be too late, Operator 5," he turned to Jimmy. "I can get no response. Evidently the lines to Buffalo are all down."

Myron Sumner! The traitor's name flashed into Jimmy Christopher's mind automatically. But why should Sumner have severed those lines? If he wanted to prevent the trap being sprung, why should he cut the wires over which the orders to cancel it must be given?

That was not logical, and yet....

Jimmy's whirling thoughts stopped short when the familiar sound of a warning siren moaned into the headquarters tent. The rocket-ships were coming! In a few minutes they would be overhead, discharging their murderous hordes to rout Colonel Walters' desperate defenders and put Batavia to the torch!

JIMMY GLANCED at his watch. It was a few minutes past noon, and a sudden suspicion dawned upon him. Springing to the door of the tent, he stepped outside and scanned the sky through field-glasses. Yes, there they were! Like trick photography on a motion-picture screen, the rocket-ships came flashing toward him—and then they were gone.

Gone not to lay waste to Batavia, but to speed on beyond it—headed straight for Buffalo! Kasuga-Tosa was going to keep his word, almost to the minute—and in his path lay Diane and Maureen with five hundred other stalwart patriots who would be needlessly slaughtered!

Somehow, the monster must be stopped! That one thought pounded through Jimmy's brain as he ran from the tent and headed for the landing field. The silver bullet-ship he had snatched from Kasuga-Tosa! It was housed in an impromptu hangar at the edge of that field—and it was his only hope, the only possible way of reaching Buffalo before disaster had swept the city and engulfed its helpless defenders!

Quickly he flung the hangar doors wide and leaped to the

door of the miniature rocket-ship, flung himself inside and grasped the controls.

With breath-taking speed the miles swept past beneath him, and then he could see Buffalo in the distance. Could see that two of the rocket-ships were hovering low in the air, over the center of the city. But where was the third? Puzzled, he swept the horizon with his eyes—and then he saw it. There was the third ship, the largest of the three, just rising from the edge of the lake and speeding to join its mates.

That was Kasuga-Tosa's flagship—and Jimmy knew all too well why it had been down there at the lakefront. The Japanese had contacted Myron Sumner; had swooped down to take the traitor and his two helpless prisoners on board. Now both Andrew Warren and Diane were on that hell-ship that must be destroyed if the ruthless invaders were to be checked before....

Desperately Operator 5 bulleted to meet them in his little ship that, compared with them, looked like an insect.

The rocket-ships saw him coming. They swung about, headed toward him, and Jimmy expected his craft to be shot down or blasted out of existence at any moment. But instead of firing upon him, Kasuga-Tosa must have given orders to disable the tiny ship. Suddenly its controls would no longer work, its combustion had stopped. Helplessly it veered around and then nosed downward, headed for the ground.

The mother-ship had taken electrical control of its fledgling, was forcing it to land, while the other two giants hovered close by like wolves eager to be in at the kill!

The moment the bullet-ship touched the ground, Jimmy

The showdown had come—and now
the battle-axes rose and fell!

flung himself at the door, determined to sell his life as dearly as possible. But the door would not open. It resisted his every effort until the rocket-ships had landed and a host of the monstrous-headed tribesmen flocked from them. Then suddenly the resistance was gone. The door flew open, and he leaped out with his automatic blazing.

But the weird-looking horde overwhelmed him. Knocking his useless weapon out of his hand, they pinioned Operator 5's arms and dragged him to where Kasuga-Tosa was alighting from his ship.

"You have gone to a great deal of trouble to rejoin me, Operator 5," the Japanese taunted when Jimmy faced him. "It would have been much simpler had you stayed with me the last time. Now we shall take precautions to see that you are not torn away from us again."

Jimmy was dragged back and lashed helplessly to an arc-light pole that stood in the center of the triangle now formed by the three ships. Out from the group at Kasuga-Tosa's side came two of the great-headed creatures who clutched long, villain-ous-looking knives. Jimmy steeled himself for what he knew was coming.

"You understand, I see." Kasuga-Tosa nodded blandly. "Let me hope that you will be wise and not prolong these proceedings any longer than necessary. You can put a stop to them at any moment by surrendering and giving me your word that you will do nothing more to organize opposition against me. If you refuse, I will have you sliced and torn into fragments!"

At his nod, the guards stepped forward, in their huge helmets and blood-red costumes, looking like weird, fantastic sacrificial priests. Their knives flickered in the sunshine and sliced through Jimmy's shirt—slit after slit. It fell away from him in ribbons, until he was bared to the waist. Once more the knives licked out at him, ran down his sides like sharp pieces of ice—leaving crimson trails in their wake....

JIMMY'S JAWS were tightly clenched. Defiantly he returned the mocking grin of the Japanese. This ordeal could not last, he told himself desperately. The rocket-ships had come down in the middle of the big square in front of the Grand Union Station. They were directly above tons of explosives that should go off at any minute.

Why didn't those mines go off? Frantically he asked himself that question as the gleaming knives came toward him again and bit into the skin at his collarbone... started to travel down his chest. Why didn't they—

The mines did not go off, but at that moment there was a dull, muffled explosion that startled even the helmeted tribes-men. That explosion came from within Kasuga-Tosa's flagship! Every eye turned toward it, to gape at the clouds of smoke now billowing from its doorways—at the smoke-blinded Japanese who came staggering out!

The flagship was on fire! Dense smoke and then a livid tongue of flame burst from the doors and ports of the lowest deck. And suddenly Jimmy knew what had happened. That explosion was the work of the American women captives on board! They had fired their own prison, and Diane was in there with them!

In the excitement Jimmy was momentarily forgotten. His

torturers dropped their knives and joined their fellows. They flung themselves at the ship, battering against its doors—only to be greeted by the point-blank fire of a heavy machine-gun when they managed to breach one.

Jimmy saw the desperate-faced girls behind that gun, and he redoubled his efforts to free himself. But the ropes which held him were tough and they had been tightly lashed. They resisted his every effort; stripped the skin from his wrists, but would not yield. Frantically he looked around him, hopelessly seeking the help he knew that he would not find... when suddenly it came to him.

Myron Sumner was there beside him—Myron Sumner, who had been standing with Mabuchi, watching those devilish torturers go to work.... Sumner there beside him with a knife, hacking and slashing at the ropes!

"I know—you don't understand this," the traitor panted, "but I am not tricking you. Maureen Durant is in that ship. Yes—" he caught the glimpse of understanding in Jimmy's eyes and admitted bitterly—"they are holding her in there. They think they are fooling me, but I know that I am being double-crossed. That rat Mabuchi wants her, and they intend to give her to him!"

Jimmy tugged and strained at the ropes, as the knife bit through them. Then the last one fell away and he was free—free to grab up one of the long knives his torturers had dropped. Straight into that milling pack he hurled himself, his keen-bladed knife slicing through those uniforms that would have resisted most bullets. Taking the invaders by surprise from the rear, they smashed their way forward, heading desperately for one of those open doors with its blazing machine-gun.

That was the only chance—and it would work! They were almost clear of the pack, had almost reached the bullet-swept runway, when Ito Mabuchi leaped in the way.

For only a fraction of a second he stood there. Then Sumner was upon him, charging him recklessly, heedlessly taking the Jap's knife in his shoulder—while his own blade whipped out in a sweeping arc that severed Mabuchi's jugular and almost decapitated him.

That desperate duel had held the center of attention. Every eye was fixed upon it, and before the spectators had recovered from their surprise, Jimmy sprang up the runway, caught the reeling Sumner and dragged him along—to fling themselves beneath the barrel of the machine-gun just as it again went into thundering action.

Once inside, Jimmy quickly took command.

"Stay with the girls. Help them hold off that pack," he snapped at Sumner, and then went racing upstairs to the control room.

As he expected, in the open doorway of that room crouched three of the liberated harem girls, their machine-gun covering the raging men inside.

"Fine work!" Jimmy applauded, as he pounded up to them. Then he faced the Japs. "Get at those controls and start this ship moving!" his crackling voice whipped out. "Move, I tell you—or you will all be blasted to hell!"

THE JAPANESE took their places at the controls—and the great ship moved, started into the air, a cloud of black smoke trailing behind it. Jimmy had been tense until that moment. Then he sighed with relief.

"Watch them," Jimmy instructed the girls, as he turned to leave. "The moment they attempt to leave those controls or that you suspect they are up to some trickery—cut them down."

Then he hurried back downstairs, to find that Sumner and the girls had released President Warren and were in complete control of the ship. They had penned up the few Japanese who remained on board, where they could do no harm. The fire was gaining headway, he noticed at once, but when he investigated he found that it was not as bad as it seemed. It could be fought, and he quickly organized a fire brigade to keep it under control.

The rocket-ship was in the air, but Jimmy saw now that the other two ships had ascended also. They were pursuing, now out in front and compelling Jimmy to turn back—crowding in, evidently intending to crush and disable the rocket-ship between them if they failed to drive it down to the square that was now thronged with their monstrous-headed slaves.

Jimmy raced back up the stairs. But when he reached the control room he halted, staring in amazement at the open-mouthed Japanese navigators. Then he saw the reason for their surprise.

There, coming toward them from the west, was a huge rocket-ship—an air-leviathan even larger than Kasuga-Tosa's craft! Straight at the flagship it came charging—and now clouds of pinkish-gray smoke billowed from it. The other two rocket-ships managed to veer away from that rapidly spreading vapor, but the flagship was enveloped in it. Jimmy did not see the spark that ignited the conflagration—but suddenly the whole outside of the ship was blazing furiously!

A flame-roaring torch, Kasuga-Tosa's huge flagship dipped and coasted desperately to the ground....

CHAPTER 12
RED DOOM

TENSE, TIGHT-JAWED, Operator 5 watched that downward plunge. This, he knew, meant certain doom for all of them—for Diane and Maureen, for Andrew Warren, Sumner and those desperate girls who had served so nobly. Now the blazing ship, surrounded by watching enemies, was dropping back into the city that would be destroyed at any moment.

But at least they would go down fighting!

"Arm yourselves!" he swiftly rallied the nonplussed girls. "Be ready with those machine-guns."

Already some of the girls had donned red coveralls that were much to large for them, were fastening the huge globular helmets over their heads. Quickly Jimmy divided them into three detachments, to be led by Andrew Warren, Sumner and himself.

Straight down into the square the flaming ship dove, to crash into the big station and half-demolish it before coming to a stop. The moment that wild drop ended, Jimmy picked himself up from the floor and led the way to one of the doors. Sumner led his detachment to another, Andrew Warren to a third. Flinging open the burning doors, they dove through the flames—and into the arms of the great-headed creatures who crowded as close as they dared come to the blazing ship.

The other two rocket-ships had landed, Jimmy saw the moment he charged out into the square. Their doors were open and their crews were joining the mob, urged on by Kasuga-Tosa, who stood on one of the runways and glowered at the mêlée with raging bloodshot eyes.

Jimmy led his weirdly caparisoned and armed detachment in a beeline toward the Japanese commander. With the machine-guns chattering at point-blank range and the fantastic-looking Oriental swords and spears laying about them on every side, the girls followed him.

Andrew Warren and Sumner saw and understood his intention. Desperately they threw their own bands in the same direction. The detachments merged—and found themselves in a trap! Kasuga-Tosa had anticipated something of this sort and was prepared for it. Out of the doorways on either side of him poured fresh hordes of the huge-headed slaves—to fling themselves on the out-matched girls and cut them down mercilessly.

Maureen Durant! Out of the corner of his eye he caught a glimpse of her. He snatched a battle-ax that had dropped from the hand of a girl at his side, and drove it through the breast of the man who had killed her. A big-headed giant towered above Maureen, was slashing down at her with a heavy sword. But at that moment Myron Sumner flung himself at the creature. Bare-handed, he grappled with the fellow and tossed him headlong.

That momentary respite gave Maureen a chance to scramble to her feet, and she stood there dazed.

"Run!" Sumner shouted. "Over there with Operator 5!"

She tried to obey, but another of the slaves cut her off. Still another bore down upon her—until suddenly Sumner catapulted himself at them, caught them both in his widely outstretched arms and imprisoned them until she had time to dart past.

For an instant he towered there in the midst of the tumult. Then his head became a battered thing, his face bathed with blood, as he went down beneath a rush of trampling feet. Myron Sumner had been a man in the end, Jimmy paid him silent tribute—a man whose life had been sadly scrambled and ruined by his inordinate ambition.

Sumner was down, his girls cut to pieces—and now Kasuga-Tosa's horde was closing in on the survivors who huddled around Jimmy and Andrew Warren.

Jimmy swung the blood-dripping ax like a flail, lashed out right and left—but he knew that this was the end. A few moments more and he would go down like Sumner....

Above him a huge bulk suddenly blotted out the light. Jimmy ducked instinctively and looked up. It was that immense newcomer ship that had swept out of the west, he recognized—and a cynical smile danced over his grim lips. Surely there was enough of them there already, without calling upon this monster to add its quota of savage killers!

But the newcomer swooped down and crashed headlong into the ship in front of Jimmy; rent and tore it like an express locomotive smashing into a runabout. And then the doors of the huge monster flew open—and out of them poured an

astonishing stream of men. Not monstrous-headed monsters—
but Americans! Americans covered with armor and wearing
tight-fitting, conical helmets with transparent visors that hung
down over their faces!

At their head was Herbert Carrol, and beside him the freckled face of Tim Donovan! In a flying phalanx those grim-faced
warriors hurled themselves toward Jimmy's sadly decimated
little party—A phalanx that swept everything before it!

LIKE TENPINS the slave-men went down, thrust back and
cut to pieces by great, heavy swords that sliced through their
red coveralls as if the material were no more than tissue paper.
In what seemed less than a moment, Jimmy was surrounded,
was being herded with Warren and the girls back toward the
air-monster.

Vainly he tried to break through that wall of friendly bodies
that barred his way. Fiercely he attempted to follow Carrol and
Tim—but those men followed their orders to the letter. They
pinioned his arms and held him helpless, while Carrol, and the
flying wedge of swordsmen who followed him, thrust their way
through the press, right up to Kasuga-Tosa's runway.

The Japanese knew that his doom was upon him at that
moment. He screamed in terror, shouted wild orders at men who
did not hear him. And then Herbert Carrol reached him—not
with the bloody-bladed sword with which he had been carving
a path. Carrol's bare hands reached out and seized the invader,
fastened in his throat and lifted Kasuga-Tosa from his feet—
swung him in the air and shook him like a great rat.

"You bloody, murdering beast!" The seething, blistering syllables chipped red-hot from his taut lips. "I swore you would get this for Bea Halliday—and I only wish I could kill you over again for every innocent life you have taken!"

Springing down from the runway where Kasuga-Tosa had met his death, Carrol led the way back to his own ship. Quickly his men followed him—up the runways in what appeared to be wild retreat.

After them came the great-headed tribesmen, driven on inexorably by their Japanese masters. Snatching for the up-drawn runways, pounding on the closed doors, they beat against the ship—until suddenly a fog of pinkish-gray gas enveloped them. A flash—and then that fog turned to crimson flame, that ate through those supposedly fire-proof uniforms, that reached out and enveloped the remaining two rocket-ships.

In less than a minute the whole square was a roaring inferno, a great bonfire—the blaze of the rocket-ships and their men mingling with the flames of the buildings they had set on fire. Nothing, it seemed, could live in that appalling conflagration. Yet strangely Carrol's ship remained in it unscathed. Like one of the rockets that propelled it, it left the ground and soared high over this city that was to go down in history as the high-water mark of Kasuga-Tosa's invasion....

"**THIS SHIP** was built in my father's factory in Akron," Carrol explained when those he had rescued gathered in his cabin. "You remember—" he smiled at Jimmy—"I told you that airplane construction was our business. I knew that something was wrong at Schenectady almost from the first. I suspected Mabuchi and Sumner but had nothing to make a case against them—not at first. Then I began to piece the thing together. I was sure of their guilt the night I discovered, as I suspected, that the plans Mabuchi had so obligingly made for us were no longer in the safe.

"I knew then that the rocket-ships were doomed to destruction before they were launched, but there was nothing I could do about it. I told Tim something of this—through the door of the storeroom in which Sumner had locked me. Tim believed me. He took a chance on me and opened the door with his skeleton key. I got away and hid out until the next day. Then I burglarized Sumner's apartment and found the plans securely tucked away under a loose floorboard.

"That's about all," he concluded. "I swore Tim to secrecy, and he soon joined me in Akron. We put thousands of men to work building this ship on Mabuchi's plans—with a few little improvements of my own; such as this gas, which will burn even a silicate composite. We kept those men locked in the factory night and day so that no word of what we were doing could leak out. We kept you in the dark, Operator 5, because we knew that Sumner was watching you—even more closely than you suspected. I was afraid that if I tried to communicate with you he would intercept the message and betray the location of our plant to Kasuga-Tosa. That was too big a risk."

"Thank God, you didn't!" Jimmy breathed fervently. "Sumner even managed to get hold of my private code. He might have intercepted anything. But what I can't understand," he puzzled, "is why our trap was not sprung—why the mines were not set off. It seems incredible that we were not all blown to pieces."

"I can answer that," Diane spoke up. "The mines were not set off because there was nobody left alive to fire them. Last night, when he left us locked in the darkness of a waterfront warehouse, Sumner went out to meet Mabuchi. Together they went from one observation post to another. Sumner pointed them out, and Mabuchi killed the crews you had stationed there—the observers and the men who were to have fired the charges when the observers gave the word."

She went on. "That note Sumner sent back to headquarters was pure bluff. He knew that the city would not be destroyed no matter what decision you made. And no matter what you had decided, I was to be handed over to Kasuga-Tosa. That much I learned when Sumner came back with Mabuchi and regaled us with a recital of his treachery."

"And that is why he cut the telephone wires and isolated Buffalo from the rest of the world—so that we would not be able to get in touch with the observation posts and learn what he had done," Jimmy Christopher added. "Well, thank God, he failed— and at last the shadow of this menace has lifted for all time."

Fervently they endorsed that sentiment—but before night his words rose up to mock at him....

BACK IN Washington, he had no more than walked into his office and dropped into his familiar, comfortable desk chair, when the telephone rang. San Francisco was on the wire.

The voice of George Keyes, the young husky whom he had ordered into the western provinces of China!

"I am the only one who is left, Operator 5," it quavered over the wire. "Willard, Burchell, Addison, Tolman—they are all dead; and I am going to be with them very soon. I have been through hell—been locked up in it for days, and now it is raging in my body. I'm a leper, Operator 5—a victim of a virulent, incurable disease!

"Don't be shocked—you are going to become very used to lepers. There are thousands of horrible cases of leprosy being propagated in China—yes, I said 'propagated.' By the Japanese government. Thousands of healthy men and women who are being inoculated with the disease. Why? So that they can bring it to America—"

Operator 5's ear rang as the reverberating bark of a shot cut short Keyes.

Silence in which Jimmy Christopher sat like a statue, staring unseeingly into space, shocked into horrified immobility by the appalling threat of this loathsome menace that was bearing down upon America—at the very moment when he had thought that at last peace and security were within the nation's grasp!

AUTHOR'S NOTE: But how frightful a toll this new scourge was to levy upon his countrymen, Operator 5 did not actually know—until the Japanese invasion, now turning to perverted medical science for its weapons, vented its full fury upon the United States. The account of that period in American history, when Jimmy Christopher and his gallant aides were called upon to perform miracles in order to stave off total annihilation, will be published in the next installment.

OPERATOR 5

- ❏ #1: The Masked Invasion — $13.95
- ❏ #2: The Invisible Empire — $13.95
- ❏ #3: The Yellow Scourge — $13.95
- ❏ #4: The Melting Death — $13.95
- ❏ #5: Cavern of the Damned — $13.95
- ❏ #6: Master of Broken Men — $13.95
- ❏ #7: Invasion of the Dark Legions — $13.95
- ❏ #8: The Green Death Mists — $13.95
- ❏ #9: Legions of Starvation — $13.95
- ❏ #10: The Red Invader — $13.95
- ❏ #11: The League of War-Monsters — $13.95
- ❏ #12: The Army of the Dead — $13.95
- ❏ #13: March of the Flame Marauders — $13.95
- ❏ #14: Blood Reign of the Dictator — $13.95
- ❏ #15: Invasion of the Yellow Warlords — $13.95
- ❏ #16: Legions of the Death Master — $13.95
- ❏ #17: Hosts of the Flaming Death — $13.95
- ❏ #18: Invasion of the Crimson Death Cult — $13.95
- ❏ #19: Attack of the Blizzard Men — $13.95
- ❏ #20: Scourge of the Invisible Death — $13.95
- ❏ #21: Raiders of the Red Death — $13.95
- ❏ #22: War-Dogs of the Green Destroyer — $13.95
- ❏ #23: Rockets From Hell — $13.95
- ❏ #24: War-Masters from the Orient — $13.95
- ❏ #25: Crime's Reign of Terror — $13.95
- ❏ #26: Death's Ragged Army — $13.95
- ❏ #27: Patriots' Death Battalion — $13.95
- ❏ #28: The Bloody Forty-five Days — $13.95
- ❏ #29: America's Plague Battalions — $13.95
- ❏ #30: Liberty's Suicide Legions — $13.95
- ❏ #31: Siege of the Thousand Patriots — $13.95
- ❏ #32: Patriots' Death March — $14.95
- ❏ #33: Revolt of the Lost Legions — $14.95
- ❏ #34: Drums of Destruction — $14.95
- ❏ #35: The Army Without a Country — $14.95
- ❏ #36: The Bloody Frontiers — $14.95
- ❏ #37: The Coming of the Mongol Hordes — $14.95
- ❏ #38: The Siege That Brought Black Death — $16.95
- ❏ #39: Revolt of the Devil Men — $16.95
- ❏ #40: The Suicide Battalion — $16.95
- ❏ #41: The Day of the Damned — $16.95
- ❏ #42: The Dawn That Shook the World — $16.95
- ❏ #43: When Hell Came to America — $16.95
- ❏ *NEW:* #44: Invasion From the Sky — $16.95

G-8 AND HIS BATTLE ACES

- ❏ #1: The Bat Staffel — $13.95

CAPTAIN COMBAT

- ❏ #1: The Sky Beast of Berlin — $13.95
- ❏ #2: Red Wings For the Blood Battalion — $13.95
- ❏ #3: Low Ceiling For Nazi Hell Hawks — $13.95

ACE G-MAN

- ❏ #1: The Suicide Squad Reports for Death — $14.95
- ❏ #2: Coffins for the Suicide Squad — $14.95
- ❏ #3: Shells for the Suicide Squad — $14.95
- ❏ #4: The Suicide Squad in Corpse-Town — $14.95
- ❏ #5: Wanted–In Three Pine Coffins — $14.95
- ❏ #6: The Suicide Squad's Dawn Patrol — $14.95
- ❏ #7: Targets for the Flaming Arrow — $16.95

DUSTY AYRES AND HIS BATTLE BIRDS

- ❏ #1: Black Lightning! — $13.95
- ❏ #2: Crimson Doom — $13.95
- ❏ #3: The Purple Tornado — $13.95
- ❏ #4: The Screaming Eye — $13.95
- ❏ #5: The Green Thunderbolt — $13.95
- ❏ #6: The Red Destroyer — $13.95
- ❏ #7: The White Death — $13.95
- ❏ #8: The Black Avenger — $13.95
- ❏ #9: The Silver Typhoon — $13.95
- ❏ #10: The Troposphere F-S — $13.95
- ❏ #11: The Blue Cyclone — $13.95
- ❏ #12: The Tesla Raiders — $13.95

MAVERICKS

- ❏ #1: Five Against the Law — $12.95
- ❏ #2: Mesquite Manhunters — $12.95
- ❏ #3: Bait for the Lobo Pack — $12.95
- ❏ #4: Doc Grimson's Outlaw Posse — $12.95
- ❏ #5: Charlie Parr's Gunsmoke Cure — $12.95

THE MYSTERIOUS WU FANG

- ❏ #1: The Case of the Six Coffins — $12.95
- ❏ #2: The Case of the Scarlet Feather — $12.95
- ❏ #3: The Case of the Yellow Mask — $12.95
- ❏ #4: The Case of the Suicide Tomb — $12.95
- ❏ #5: The Case of the Green Death — $12.95
- ❏ #6: The Case of the Black Lotus — $12.95
- ❏ #7: The Case of the Hidden Scourge — $12.95

THE SECRET 6

- ❏ #1: The Red Shadow — $13.95
- ❏ #2: House of Walking Corpses — $13.95
- ❏ #3: The Monster Murders — $13.95
- ❏ #4: The Golden Alligator — $13.95

CAPTAIN ZERO

- ❏ #1: City of Deadly Sleep — $13.95
- ❏ #2: The Mark of Zero! — $13.95
- ❏ #3: The Golden Murder Syndicate — $13.95

RED FINGER

- ❏ #1: Second-Hand Death — $24.95

www.ingramcontent.com/pod-product-compliance
Lightning Source LLC
Chambersburg PA
CBHW020331260626
47156CB00004B/1472